"Like Old Times"
An M/M Gay Romance

Max Hudson

This book is intended for Adults (ages 18+) only. The contents may be offensive to some readers. It may contain graphic language, explicit sexual content, and adult situations. May contain scenes of unprotected sex. Please do not read this book if you are offended by content as mentioned above or if you are under the age of 18.

Please educate yourself on safe sex practices before making potentially life-changing decisions about sex in real life. If you're not sure where to start, see here: http://www.jerrycoleauthor.com/safe-sex-resources/ (courtesy of Jerry Cole).

This story is a work of fiction. Names, characters, businesses, places, events and incidents are the products of the author's imagination or used in a fictitious manner and are not to be construed as real. Any resemblance to actual persons, living or dead, or actual events is purely coincidental. Products or brand names mentioned are trademarks of their respective holders or companies. The cover uses licensed images and are shown for illustrative purposes only. Any person(s) that may be depicted on the cover are simply models.

Edition v1.00 (2021.04.26)
http://www.maxhudsonauthor.com

Special thanks to the following volunteer readers who helped with proofreading: Jon Niehus, Bob, RB, Big Kidd, Blue Savannah, and those who assisted but wished to be anonymous. Thank you so much for your support.

Prologue

It was the most important night in Jim Hartnett's life, but not just because it was prom. Frankly, he had never cared much for school. The whole idea of this night being the culmination of something special seemed forced. While school may have been special for people who actually cared and were part of the community, for Jim it was a place of pain and anguish, where he had been an outsider, forever destined to gaze into a life he could never have. For other people life seemed to be simple. They knew how to act and how to live together without being awkward. They had people to rely on, to trust.

It wasn't like that for Jim.

For years he'd had a secret that he held close to his heart, so close that the effort of holding onto it made him tremble. Letting this secret out was too much of a risk so he had held his tongue and made sure that he didn't stand out at all at school so that he would never be placed under scrutiny. Some people may have thought him odd and strange for spending so much time alone, but he didn't care. If they really knew him, they would only ridicule him and ensure that he had a terrible time. The bullies were always quick to pick on anyone they saw as vulnerable.

But tonight, things were going to change. As Jim buttoned up his shirt and tightened his purple tie around his slender neck he breathed out, collecting his nerves. He brushed a few errant strands of his sandy blonde hair away from his face and looked at his reflection. Having just turned 18 he was losing the flush of youth. Whispers of stubble swept across his jaw, and his eyes were becoming harder as they attuned to the world. Soon enough he would be a man properly, venturing out into the world.

His father, Malcolm, had recently sat Jim down for a rare conversation about the passage of time and the state of the world. It was mostly an awkward thing where Malcolm had stumbled through the speech, but one thing he said had struck a chord with Jim.

'This is the most important time in your life because it's the time when you're going to choose the man you're going to become. In school you can get away with certain things and you have a safety net, but that's not true when you get out there. The world doesn't owe you any favors and it's not going to give you any, so you have to decide who you're going to be by what you do and how you treat people. Your actions are going to be what defines you, and it begins now.'

They were stirring words, which was surprising coming from his father, who always seemed so uncertain about his role in the world. But Jim knew exactly who he wanted to be. He wanted to be someone that was brave, someone that was going to make a difference in the world, someone that was going to go after what he wanted and not be defined by his fear.

Prom was the night that was all going to change.

Of course he didn't have a date for the prom, much to his parent's dismay. He would tell them why later though, but tonight he wanted to share his secret with the person who meant the most to him in the world: Mike. Just the thought of his name made a warm feeling sweep through Jim's body. A haze rippled through his mind and a knot tightened in the pit of his stomach. A smile appeared on his face, but it faded quickly. Jim could see the uncertainty in his own eyes. Revealing a secret like this could destroy a friendship, but Jim had held it within his heart for so long now if he didn't release it into the world he was going to explode. Mike was the only person who had made school tolerable. He was Jim's best friend, and over the past few years Jim had fallen deeply, madly in love with Mike.

It was his smile, his laugh, the curl of his lip and the way he tilted his head when he was listening to something Jim said. It was in his dark mane of hair, as thick as a forest, and the hard angles of his body. It was in his sensual eyes and in all the moments they had spent together over the years. Love had blossomed inside Jim's heart, probably even before he knew what love truly was, but he had kept it to himself. At first it was because he didn't fully understand what was happening himself, but then it became dangerous. He knew that if he told Mike the truth it would change their friendship irrevocably, and something precious would be lost. But Jim didn't want to be the kind of man who was afraid to take risks, so on this night he intended to tell Mike the truth and see what happened. He wasn't sure if Mike felt the same way or not, or if Mike was even gay. There were moments when it seemed impossible that Mike didn't love him, but then Jim knew that he was seeing things from a biased perspective and he probably shouldn't trust his own judgment in these matters. But he had to tell Mike what was happening. He simply couldn't go on otherwise. School was ending. It was the beginning of a new era, and Jim was hoping the era would be defined by love.

***

Mike swung by in his beat-up car that was his pride and joy. He beeped the horn and swept his arm through the air, gesturing for Jim to join him. Jim squealed with delight and ran out of the house, shouting a quick goodbye to his parents. There was a warning to be home at a reasonable time and a wish that he enjoyed himself, but the words were already fading into the distance as Jim raced to join Mike in the car. As soon as he was in the passenger seat the engine roared and the car sped away. Mike always looked so in control when he drove. He wore a suit too, and had a matching purple tie, but somehow Jim thought it looked better on him. He was just a few months older than Jim, but he had always been more mature and seemed to know innately how to do certain things and how to make his way in the world. It was something that Jim admired about him, and something that attracted him. Jim's gaze drifted down to Mike's lips and wondered if, by the end of the night, he would be tasting a sweet, honeyed kiss.

"What are you starting at? Do I have something on my face?" Mike asked.

"No," Jim replied, averting his gaze swiftly. Blood rushed to his cheeks and he gazed out of his window, watching the blurred world rush by. "I was just thinking about tonight and what a big fuss everyone else is making of it."

"I know right. I don't know why they think it's going to be the most important night of our lives. We have so many years left. I hope that I'm going to be doing something important enough that high school isn't the highlight of my life. God, can you imagine if we peaked here?" he barked a laugh and shook his head at the thought. Jim laughed too.

"I think it's safe to say that we're going to do better in the real world than we ever did in school."

"Yeah, it's certainly going to be an adventure," Mike said. There was an undercurrent of emotion to his words that Jim detected, but Mike didn't elaborate and Jim didn't delve further into the subject. It was only a short drive to school and soon enough they were pulling into the parking lot, which was already filled with fellow students. The boys were dressed smartly, while the girls were all wearing colorful dresses, having also adorned themselves with sparkling jewelry. Jim noticed the couples that stood around, sharing intimate whispers and a secret language. He swallowed a lump in his throat and tried to quell the feeling of envy that crept up from his heart. He wondered if they knew how lucky they were.

Prom ended up being much like their school life had been. Jim and Mike stood on the sidelines, making sarcastic jokes and amusing themselves while the rest of the school seemed to be in a separate bubble. Jim watched on as people danced slowly together, holding each other tightly as the music cocooned them in an intimate haze. He stole surreptitious glances at Mike, the words lodged in his throat.

Would you like to dance? It was just five simple words, a simple question that might change things forever. But no, it wasn't time yet. Jim had to do this properly. He had rehearsed what he was going to say over and over again, and if events unspooled as they did in his mind then the night was going to have a very happy ending.

"You know, I've been thinking about this a lot and I don't think I'm going to miss this place at all," Mike said, gazing idly out at the sea of people on the dance floor.

"Are you sure about that? It might be different once we're actually out of here," Jim said.

"No, I'm pretty sure, I mean, the only person I give a damn about is you and we're still going to keep in touch. Everyone else…nah," Mike said with a curt shake of the head. "What have they ever done for me? They can all go and live their lives. I doubt I'll see anyone else here again. And as for the lessons, well, I've never really felt like I've belonged here. I've always felt that this is kind of a place where we've had to wait for our real lives to begin. I'm anxious to get out there and see what adventures are waiting for me."

"I'm sure it's going to be something great," Jim said, admiring the way Mike was ready and willing to charge headlong into the unknown no matter the dangers.

"Maybe," Mike said, sipping his drink. The word seemed heavier than it should have been, and Jim sensed that there was something Mike wasn't telling him. Before he could ask him about it though the music stopped and the principal strode out on stage, wishing everyone a good prom and making a small speech. He then crowned the King and Queen of the prom, which surprised nobody as it was the math genius Toby Winters and the hardworking school president Hayley Burns. They strode up on stage and clasped hands, celebrating their achievements. They looked so proud, and Jim couldn't help but wonder what it would be like to stand on a stage like that and proclaim his love to the world. He glanced toward Mike and smiled. If this were some movie this was the part where Jim would rush through the crowd and take over the stage, and then declare his love for Mike for all to hear. The crowd would part like the Red Sea and then he and Mike would meet on the dance floor as music rose all around them in a fanfare.

But this was not a movie, and Jim was not the kind of person to make such a dramatic gesture. Besides, he didn't want anyone else to be involved in this. It was none of their business. Mike's was the only opinion that mattered.

The night drew on and the hours grew small. Eventually Mike and Jim had had their fill of prom.

"Come on, let's get back to the car and we'll go somewhere better than this. We've made an appearance and we can now say that we have been to prom. I don't think we're going to get much else from the night," Mike said. He was already leaving. Jim naturally followed. Butterflies fluttered in his stomach and his heart raced as he knew the moment was approaching when he was going to confess his feelings for Mike. Before this he had been determined to share his feelings, but the closer the moment came, the more nervous he became. His throat ran dry and wild thoughts ran through his mind. He wondered if he should save it for another day. After all, it was getting late and maybe he should wait until they were somewhere more comfortable.

Excuses danced with reasons in his mind and he was trying to justify to himself why he should leave it. But then he clenched his fists into tight balls.

NO.

The thought thundered through his mind. He had worked himself up too much for this. This was one of the moments that was going to define his life, and he wasn't going to let it slip away. He needed to tell Mike the truth, otherwise he was never going to be able to take risks.

They drove out to Lookout Point, a small section of a park that looked over the city. It was a popular place with the local youth, although on prom night there were few cars parked along the crescent edge of the cliff. Tall trees stood around them, offering privacy from the narrow winding road. Mike and Jim clambered out of the car and perched on the hood, resting their backs against the windshield. The night sky stretched out above them, an infinity of stars. The city below shone brightly, glittering as though it was reflecting the sky above it. It was a place that thrived with life, but none of that mattered to Jim. In amongst all the souls that lived in the city were the two of them, and in that moment the rest of the world melted away.

"It's so massive isn't it," Mike said in a low whisper.

"What is?"

"The universe. When you look up at the stars, it just goes on and on and on. You ever think we're going to know what's out there?"

"I don't know. Probably not, at least not in our lifetime."

"I guess you're right. It's a shame though. Sometimes if you look long enough you can start to see the future."

"Oh yeah? And what do you see in your future?"

Mike pressed his lips together and took a few moments before he answered. "I'm not sure. Something that makes a difference in people's lives."

"That would be a noble cause. I just want to be happy," Jim said. He stared at the stars and saw them shift and transform. He wondered if it was a sign. He turned his head to look at Mike, gazing at the profile of his face. In the dim moonlight he looked almost ethereal, as though he was a being not of this earth. Every fiber of Jim's body trembled with desire. It would have been so easy for him to reach across and caress Mike's cheek, to sidle over and feel their warm breath mingle, but first Jim had to say the words that burned in his mind. His chest rose with deep breaths as he summoned the courage.

"Mike," he began, the word as sharp as glass in his throat, but as he said this Mike had already turned to face him and was speaking himself.

"There's something I need to talk to you about Jim," he said, and apparently, he hadn't registered what Jim said.

"Okay," Jim said, the word catching in his throat as he waited. There was always time to tell Mike again.

Mike looked pensive, although perhaps it was just the moonlight. "I don't know how to tell you this, but there is something I do know about my future. I've been thinking about what to do after school for a long time and honestly the prospects scared me. I mean, I've known for a long time that I've never been smart enough to go to college, and I'm not sure what type of job I'd be good at. But there's one thing that I think I've always been destined for. I know we said we'd keep in touch after high school, but I'm going to have to leave for a while. We might not see each other for a long time."

"What do you mean? Where are you going?" Jim asked, furrowing his brow.

"I've signed up to the army. I'll ship out right after graduation," he said.

Jim felt as though he had been punched in the gut. Color drained from his face. All he could do was nod numbly.

"Oh... okay," he stammered. "But why? You know what they're doing out there isn't right. Why wouldn't you tell me about this sooner?"

"Because I knew you'd react like this. I know how you feel about the military and I'm not saying it's perfect, but it's been a tradition in my family and I think it's important that it's continued. It's hard for you to understand I know, but this is something I feel I have to do. It makes sense to me. If there's anything like destiny in the world then I think this is it. I'm sorry, I know I should have told you sooner I just never found the right time. You're my best friend though and you're the only person who got me through high school."

The words glazed over Jim's mind and instead anger rose within him, mixed with betrayal. He sat up and then swung his legs off the car, pacing around to try and work off the anxious energy. He swept a hand through his hair and looked toward Mike with confusion.

"How can you do this Mike? You know what we're doing out there is wrong. The army isn't what it used to be. There's no honor in dying for oil," Jim said, his words so passionate that he was always shouting. Mike remained calm and looked at him with impassivity.

"I don't want to argue with you about this Jim. It's already decided. I'm going. Please, I don't want my last memories of you to be of us arguing."

"I don't care what you want!" Jim cried. "You can't do this Mike. You can't just leave. We... we had so many plans. We were going to do so many things together. Come on, you can call them and back out. It's still not too late. You can change this. You don't have to do this. We can find you a job that you're suited to and you'll be good at it, I promise. You can do something safer. Mike, please, I hate the thought of you going out there. What if you… what if you…" Jim couldn't bring himself to finish the sentence. He gasped and clutched his stomach. It felt as though his heart was being ripped out. Mike slid across the hood of the car.

"Nothing is going to happen Mike. I'm going to do my tour and learn a few skills, and then I'm going to return better than ever. And when I do, we'll come out here and hang out just like old times, okay?" Mike said. When Jim didn't respond Mike climbed off the car and wrapped a hand around the back of Jim's neck, pulling him closer into an embrace. "Okay?" he repeated. Jim was suddenly swarmed with Mike's musky, masculine scent. This wasn't supposed to be how it happened. Jim was supposed to tell Mike that he loved him. This was supposed to be the night when they got together, when their happy ending could begin, but instead it was just the beginning of a nightmare.

And Jim couldn't do anything to stop it. There was no point telling Mike the truth now. What would it change? It would only make things hurt more. Mike had made up his mind. The papers had been signed and fate had been put into motion. Mike was going to leave him. The person who meant the most to him in the world was disappearing. He was filled with a lurching sensation, as though the world was shifting around him and he had no idea how to stop it.

"I don't know what I'm going to do without you," Jim said in choking breaths.

"You're going to be fine. You can do anything you want to do," Mike said. Jim didn't say anything in response, he simply clung to Mike in the hope that if he never let go then Mike wouldn't have to leave him. But of course that wasn't the case. He ended up returning home with red and swollen eyes. He cried and thumped his pillow with anguish, afraid that he would never see Mike again, afraid that his love would always be fleeting.

Chapter One

Mike looked out at the dusty desert that had been his world for the past four years. Sometimes it seemed impossible that so much time had passed. The world had left him behind. It kept spinning and the peacekeeping forces in the Middle East seemed destined to stay there. Over the course of the past four years he had been promoted and was part of a good squad, and sometimes he forgot that he had another home. The truck rumbled along the gritty road. In the distance bland buildings rose up, peppering the landscape like ruins. He looked at the world with pity, and even though he wore his uniform with pride there were moments when he wondered what he was doing out here. He tried to not think about it too much though lest he descend into insanity.

"What movie do you want to watch later tonight?" Aaron asked. The hulking soldier with midnight skin grinned at Mike.

"Something with some action in. I'm getting tired of all the soppy romantic ones you've been picking lately," Mike replied.

"Hey, if you want to pick the movie then you just have to beat me at poker. It's not my fault that you can't bluff worth a damn," Aaron's voice was low and rumbling. Mike smirked and looked at him through hooded eyes.

"Yeah, well, I think we could use a change, that's all."

"You're not getting enough action out here?" Aaron teased.

"Oh yeah, going to these outposts and defusing bombs always gets the adrenalin pumping," Mike said sarcastically, gazing toward the low-roofed buildings that were difficult to distinguish from the rest of the sandy backdrop.

"Hey, what's gotta be done has to be done. But look, if it means that much to you then I'll choose something with a bit more fire, it's not like we end up watching the movie anyway." There was a playfulness in Aaron's eyes that made Mike's heart dance. This was a bland, forsaken world, but it wasn't empty of its delights either.

"You have a deal," Mike said, looking forward to later.

The army hadn't been exactly what he imagined it would be when he signed up, but it had been a transformative experience and he knew he wouldn't have been the same man had he remained at home. He was a better man now, stronger, and he had made bonds with people that would never be broken. It reminded him of the friendship he'd had with Jim. Guilt flared in his heart, for he had promised Jim that he would return home, but he'd signed up for another tour as his first one had ended, and since communication was sketchy it was difficult to keep in touch with home. He told himself that people changed and drifted apart all the time, but he wasn't sure it made it any easier.

"Incoming!" the warning cry interrupted his thoughts and it almost came too late. Mike glanced out of the window and saw a plume of smoke rushing through the sky just as the impact hit them, reverberating through the truck. The truck pitched forward. Glass shattered and chaos reigned.

"It's a damned trap!" a voice called out.

"Get out! Assume defensive positions! They've been waiting for us!"

The truck was suddenly peppered with the rat a tat of machine gun fire. Mike bent his head low and kicked the door open, firing back a few shots to offer himself cover as he tumbled out and made his way around. Aaron was just behind him. The trucks had come to a stop. Another missile was fired and it took out one of the jeeps in a blazing inferno. Mike was haunted by the screams of the dying in amongst the crackling flames. The squad leader gave them orders to circle around and pick off the insurgents. Covering fire was laid down. Mike and Aaron raced toward the jeep that was on fire. The air shimmered with heat and uncomfortable sweat trickled underneath his gear.

"This is why I don't pick action movies," Aaron said through gritted teeth. Obscured by the flames, Mike pointed to a rising building that would hopefully give them a better angle. He just had to hope that they were quick enough to avoid the shots that were coming their way. He counted down from three and then Aaron laid down covering fire. Mike's heart pounded as he pressed himself flat against the sand wall. He waved Aaron forward. Mike leaned around and squeezed the trigger, feeling the reverberations of the gun against his bicep. He beckoned Aaron forward, eager to get the man to safety, but then Aaron's expression turned to one of horror. Mike heard a gunshot behind him and saw the bullet spear into Aaron's neck. Blood spurted out in a spray of red mist and Aaron crumpled to the ground. Mike swung around, roaring as he shot. His bullet killed the insurgent, but not before the insurgent managed to get another shot away. Mike felt the fire burn inside him. It took a few moments for him to realize that the deafening scream was his own. He collapsed to the ground and when he pressed his hand against his side it came back stained with blood, but his only thought was for Aaron. He looked back to see the crumpled body stretched limply over the ground, the eyes lifeless and glassy.

"No…" Mike choked as he winced, trying to keep pressure on his wound, but the strength left him and the world grew hazy. He tried to keep his eyes open but it was so difficult… so difficult.

Eventually there was only darkness.

***

Mike opened his eyes, expecting to see the sapphire blue sky and to feel the scratchy sand underneath him. Instead, he was on a comfortable bed and above him was a white ceiling. He gazed around and groaned when he realized he was in a hospital ward. Sighing, he tried to move, but pain seized his body. He grunted and gasped as he struggled, as a doctor appeared before him. She was short, with straight black hair and slightly tanned skin. Her name was Dr. Lopez, and from the tone of her voice he got the impression that she was not to be messed with.

"It's good to have you back with us, how are you feeling?" she asked, examining his chart.

"Like I want to get out of here," he said. She smirked, as though she had heard that many times before.

"Yes, well, unfortunately I don't think that's going to happen for a little while yet."

"Why not?" he asked, his voice gritty and defensive.

"Because the bullet that punctured your skin went right through, grazing your spine and damaging your nerves. You should be able to walk again, but it's going to be a long, hard road, and you're going to need time to recover."

"What?" Mike asked, furrowing his brow. This wasn't supposed to happen. This wasn't the kind of thing that was supposed to happen to him. It had just been a routine mission. Why had things gone so wrong? Suddenly he remembered Aaron.

"What about Aaron? I mean, corporal Jones, Aaron Jones. Please. He was shot. He…" Mike trailed off when he remembered that fateful moment as Aaron had been shot through the neck. The spraying blood had been like a fountain.

"I'm afraid we don't have someone of that name here," Dr. Lopez said. Mike leaned back in his pillow, knowing why Aaron wasn't there. God. The line between death and life was so thin, as was the thread that tethered them to this world.

"What's going to happen to me now?" he asked, his voice dry and scratchy. Dr. Lopez seemed to notice as she poured him a glass of water and handed it to him. He got the impression that it was an order for him to drink it.

"We're going to keep you here for a few days to keep an eye on your progress, and then you'll be shipping home. Someone else will be along to tell you all about that and how you can apply for military benefits and welfare if you need it. I'm hoping that with enough determination you won't see a significant drop in your mobility."

"If there's not going to be a significant drop then I can get back out there," Mike said. *And get revenge on the bastards who killed Aaron.*

"Significant for the normal world, not out here. You wouldn't be able to pass a medical examination to serve in the army again. I'm sorry. I know it's going to take you a little time to get used to this. Now that you're awake though I can get you a tablet. You can watch a movie or something. Any requests?"

Mike thought about it and closed his eyes. "Something romantic," he said, clenching his jaw as he tried to stop tears from seeping out of his eyes.

Chapter Two

"I like these ones," Jim said, picking up two bunny ornaments. One of them was standing on its hind legs, looking up as though it was sniffing a flower, while the other was hunched over, searching the ground for a treat. Ryan shook his head and placed his hand on his hip.

"Bunnies are cute around easter, but I don't want our ornaments to be seasonal. I want them to fit all year round. Come on, I saw some nice ones over here," he said, placing his hand on Jim's shoulder to guide him through the store. They walked to another aisle and Jim arched his eyebrow when he saw the abstract shapes that Ryan wanted.

"Okay, you might not want seasonal things, but I at least want something that I can understand," Jim said, folding his arms.

"What's not to understand about this? This is not just an ornament, this is an adventure. Every time you look at it, you'll see something different. It will lead us to the realm of the abstract and open our minds to new possibilities and new ideas," Ryan's blue eyes shimmered as he stood beside the ornament, but Jim just laughed.

"I'm not having *that* in our lounge," he said, and then sighed. "Who knew that decorating our place was going to be this much work?"

"I thought it was going to be more fun than this. Where's your sense of flair darling?" Ryan teased, kissing Jim on the cheek.

"Maybe we should take a break from this and go get a bite to eat," Jim suggested, and Ryan readily agreed. They went to the café in the store and each got a coffee and a slice of cake to share. They had recently moved into an apartment together and were in the process of decorating it, but were finding difficulty in choosing something they were both happy with. Jim understood the need to compromise in relationships, but he wanted something that he could at least tolerate. This was all still new to him though. Ryan was his first serious boyfriend and the idea of moving in together was exciting. The reality was still exciting, although less so as it was mired in the drudgery of the mundane.

"Don't worry Jim, we'll get there eventually. There are plenty of other stores and plenty of other ornaments. We'll find the perfect one."

"I hope so. I don't want our place to be empty because we couldn't ever agree on anything."

"Oh shush you, you're always looking at the negative. Now, while we're out should we get something to take to your parents?" Ryan asked.

Jim shrugged. "I mean, we can if you want, but we're just popping over there for dinner. It's not really a big occasion or anything."

Ryan leaned over the table and placed his hand on Jim's. "Every moment spent with your parents is a big occasion. At least it is for me. I want to make a good impression on them. I still don't think your mom likes me."

"Oh you're just being paranoid. She likes you just fine," Jim said. Ryan remained unconvinced.

"I don't know, whenever we're together I get the feeling that she's waiting for me to trip up on something or say the wrong thing. And she looks at me so strangely. I just don't know how I'm supposed to act when I'm around her."

"Oh, just be yourself," Jim said, smiling widely. "You're really making a problem out of nothing. Believe me, Mom would say something if she had a problem with you."

"Would she really?"

"Yes, she's not the type of person to hold things back. So, you have nothing to worry about. All she wants is for me to be happy, and I am happy with you, so she won't have any problem," Jim said, hoping that his words would reassure Ryan. He leaned across the table and enjoyed a sweet kiss, and Ryan did look more at ease.

"Okay, okay, I will try to believe that everything is right with the world and that I don't have anything to worry about. But I still think we should pick up some cookies or something just to grease the wheels. I can't stand anyone not liking me, especially not the parents of my lover," he stressed the last word and lowered his eyes, giving Jim a sultry gaze.

Jim laughed. "If you want a tip then don't refer to me as your lover while she's around. My folks are still quite traditional in some ways," he said. Ryan winked at him and agreed that discretion was valuable in some instances.

Jim sipped his coffee and reflected on the man that was sitting before him. When Ryan had first come up to him, Jim had been intimidated by Ryan's confidence and carefree attitude, but Ryan had quickly won him over and the two had been an item ever since. Things had progressed quickly and Jim was comfortable with Ryan, although there was a sense that a certain something was missing. Jim told himself that he was just being silly, and that it wasn't fair to compare Ryan to something that could never be. The simple fact was that Mike still played on his mind and it had caused other relationships to crash and burn. Jim always wanted to feel something similar to what he felt for Mike, but it was impossible. With Ryan he wanted to break out of this cycle. There was no point being hung up on Mike. That ship had never left port, and it never would. Mike was out there in some forsaken part of the world fighting for the flag, and from what Jim heard he wasn't planning to come back any time soon.

They had lost touch pretty quickly after Mike had gone overseas. The communication was patchy and Jim had intentionally delayed his replies as it was too painful to speak with him without being with him. That summer had been the worst of Jim's life, and there were moments when he hadn't been sure he would pull through. But that was four years ago now. He was with Ryan and the future was looking bright. There was no reason to let his unrequited love for Mike tarnish what was developing with Ryan, no reason at all.

***

After they finished up at the store they drove to Jim's parent's house. He knocked on the door before opening it and walking in. Malcolm sat in front of the TV, watching the football game, while Jenny was in the kitchen baking. She wandered out sucking some cake mix off her thumb and greeted Jim with a hug. She was more cordial with Ryan, who smiled and handed her the cookies they had picked up. Jenny thanked them.

"Did you have any success today?" she asked.

Jim and Ryan glanced at each other and laughed. "It's still a work in progress. We're just narrowing down our choices until we get to the real kernel of aesthetic beauty," Jim said.

Jenny rolled her eyes. "If you say so," she said. "Would you like a sandwich or anything?" she asked. Both Ryan and Jim said they would love one. Ryan glanced at the TV and walked toward Malcolm, inquiring about the score. Jim had never been one for sports and in some ways, he regretted it because it was a big passion of his father's and something they would have been able to share, but Ryan liked sports and it gave him something to bond with Malcolm about. Jim was about to follow them when Jenny asked him to join her in the kitchen.

He followed his mom and helped her make the sandwiches. Watching her in the kitchen was like being in the presence of a master at work. Somehow, she made even the most ordinary dishes taste magical, and he had never been able to learn her secret.

"So, you and Ryan are getting pretty serious then?" she asked.

"Yeah, I mean, moving in together is a big step, but we have a lot of fun together and we take care of each other," he said.

"That's good," she replied quietly.

When Ryan had confessed his concerns to Jim, Jim had dismissed them for the sake of reassuring him, but secretly he was a little concerned with the way his mom acted.

"Mom, Ryan is a little worried that you don't like him," Jim ventured, hoping that his mom would turn around and act shocked as though she couldn't believe that she had ever given that impression. It was somewhat worrying when silence lingered in the air. "Mom?" Jim ventured, stretching out the word.

Jenny sliced a sandwich and sighed, turning to face him. "It's not that I dislike Ryan. I think he's a kind young man with a good head on his shoulders, but I do wonder if he's the right person for you. I want you to be happy, and I want you to be in love. I want you to be with someone who you feel you can't live without."

"What makes you think that's not Ryan?" Jim asked, perplexed by her attitude.

"I've seen you in love before Jim and this isn't it."

Jim recoiled and suddenly became defensive. "What do you mean? I haven't been in love before. What are you talking about?"

Jenny smiled. "Jim, I'm your mother. I knew you were gay long before you told us and I also know your moods. I know it hurt you when Mike left and I just want to make sure you're going into this relationship with everything out in the open. There can be no room for dishonesty in love. If you're going to be with someone then you have to make sure that you want to be with them above all others, otherwise it's not fair to them. I'm just a little worried that you're doing all this because you think it's the right thing to do and because you're afraid of being alone. Don't think I haven't noticed that Ryan has been the driving force behind all of this."

Jim was indignant. "I really like Ryan! We're good together."

"I'm not saying you're not. I just want to make sure that he's the best person for you."

Jim's cheeks burned at the knowledge that Jenny knew about his love for Mike. Back then it had seemed like such a huge secret he was carrying by himself. It had never occurred to him that someone else might see the truth.

"How did you know that I loved Mike?"

"It was written all over your face every time you saw him. A mother knows these things," Jenny said kindly.

"Well, I can tell you that I am well and truly over him. It's not like it matters anyway. Mike has his own life now and from what I understand I don't think he's going to be coming back any time soon."

"Didn't you hear? Mike is back," Jenny said. The words were like a thunderclap. Jim's blood turned to ice.

"What?"

"Yeah, there was some accident out there so he's back with Hank and Michelle. He got back about a week ago. Sorry, I assumed that he'd get in touch with you."

"No, he didn't," Jim said, and he couldn't help but feel a little betrayed. "Is he all right? What happened to him?"

"I think he's fine. He just has a bit of trouble walking that's all. Perhaps you should see him. I'm sure he'd appreciate a visit."

Jim nodded, still stunned by the news. He had gotten so used to the idea of never seeing Mike again that it was surreal thinking he was back at home. Jim's stomach curdled with anticipation about seeing him. But did Mike even want to see him? Was he angry that Jim hadn't made enough effort to keep in touch? Why hadn't he tried to get in touch with Jim? So many years had passed and Jim wasn't sure what that meant for their friendship, but underneath all this doubt and anxiety he was certain of one thing; he was excited to see Mike again. It was a dangerous thing though because he could feel all the old feelings that he had pushed down deep into the abyss of his soul rising once again. He took the sandwiches into the front room and handed one to Ryan, wondering how he was going to feel about all this.

***

"Are you okay? You seem distracted," Ryan said as they departed from Malcolm and Jenny's house.

"I'm okay, it's just been a long day, you know," Jim said with a smile. He turned the volume of the radio down, trying to ignore the thrum in his mind. The news that Mike had returned had shaken him to his core. "By the way, just to set your mind at ease I did ask Mom if she had a problem with you and she told me to tell you that you have absolutely nothing to worry about."

"Oh God, you told her? She's going to think that I'm some kind of paranoid wreck now," Ryan whined, tapping the steering wheel nervously with his index finger. When he was in this mood his long face looked even longer, drooping down as though it was melting wax. He gnawed on his lower lip and sighed. "Well, I guess there's nothing else for it except to hope things get better in time. Once we have the place set up, we'll invite them over for dinner and they can see us in our natural habitat. I'm sure things will be easier then," he said. "I prefer spending time with your Dad. He's so much more... uncomplicated. I can talk about football with him and I don't ever have to wonder about where I stand."

"Uncomplicated is certainly one word to describe him," Jim said. "There's something else that I want to talk to you about as well. Do you remember Mike?"

"Mike…" Ryan said, letting the world linger on his tongue. "Ah, was he your friend at high school?"

Friend was putting it mildly. Jim hadn't told Ryan the true extent of his feelings for Mike. He hadn't seen any point in dredging up the past and now, well, perhaps it was a little dishonest but it seemed like it was going to make things more complicated than they needed to be. Both he and Mike were different people. There was no chance of things being as they were.

"Yeah, well, remember I told you that we lost touch when he signed up for the army? Well, apparently he's back in town. I was thinking of paying him a visit. You wouldn't mind, would you?"

"Of course not. I mean, while I am philosophically opposed to the army as a systemic issue with our country, I can hardly take that out on the people who go out there and fight. I see them more as victims really, slaves to the propaganda machine that keeps chewing up bodies and sending them back here as broken people."

"Yeah… well, hopefully he isn't broken," Jim said. He didn't know what to expect when he saw Mike, but it was going to be a momentous occasion. There were so many things bubbling inside him, things he thought he was never going to have an opportunity to say. Was now the right time, or was it pointless to return to the past in that manner? His mind was filled with questions and when he returned home he wanted to spend some time alone in the hope of figuring out his conflicted feelings. Was his mom right? Was he just settling for Ryan because it was comfortable and it was easy to let Ryan take charge of the course of their relationship? Just because things were different with him than his feelings were for Mike it didn't mean that his feelings for Ryan meant nothing... didn't it?

Love was so confusing and sometimes he wished he were a monk. At least then all he'd have to worry about was being devout enough to get into heaven.

Chapter Three

"Dinner's ready Mike!" Michelle called.

"I'll take it in here," Mike called out.

There was a pause. "I really think it's better if you come and sit at the table with us," she said.

"My leg is hurting. I'd rather stay here." Mike could hear the murmurs exchanged between his parents. He sighed and ignored the stabbing pain in his chest where his heart used to be. That organ had been left back in the Middle East, resting next to Aaron. Mike was in his bed, in his old room, surrounded by the posters that had been erected when he was a teenager. It was as though he had gone back in time, but only he had changed. This place was a time capsule of history, his history, a life that no longer existed, a person that had long since ceased to be. Images flickered on the TV that he was half-watching. The branches of a tree brushed against the window, making it sound as though some monster was scratching to get in. When he was a kid Mike used to be terrified of that sound, but he wasn't any longer. He knew that the true monsters of the world all had human faces.

Michelle came in with the tray and laid it beside him, placing his drink on his bedside cabinet.

"Are you okay? Do you need any tablets?"

"No, I'm fine. I just want to rest my leg," he said. Michelle nodded, her features looking pinched. Every time Mike looked at her, he was filled with guilt because he knew what a burden he was placing on them. Next to his bedside cabinet were his cane and his crutches. He had both as the pain in his leg differed in its intensity from day to day, and oh how he hated the predictability of it.

"Okay, we would like you to eat dinner with us though. We've missed having you there over the years. It's a good way for us to share what's happened during the day."

Mike grunted a dry laugh. "I don't get up to anything interesting in here," he said.

"I know, but it's still good to talk. Listen, I'm popping to the store later. I think you should come. It would be good for you to get some fresh air and maybe see a few people," she said.

Mike was about to tell her that he wanted to stay in bed when she clasped his hand tightly. Her voice was terse and she looked at him intently, her eyes swimming with pain. "I really want you to come Mike. I'm not going to order you or anything like that, but I hate thinking of you cooped up in here all this time. It's not good for you. You're coming with me," she said. Mike didn't want to be an eternal disappointment to her so he nodded. She left him to eat his dinner, and then afterwards it was time to leave.

There was always at least a dull ache in his leg, but he felt guilty every time he complained because at least he was still around to feel pain. So many others had lost their lives, including Aaron. When Mike had returned to the world, he wasn't entirely sure what he had been fighting for. The country had not prospered in his absence and nobody thought highly of the war. Nobody treated him like a hero. He gripped his cane as he stepped out of the car and walked alongside his mother. The store was busy and Mike felt a twitch in his stomach. Ever since he'd returned home, he hated being in crowds. They were loud and noisy, unpredictable. At least at home he could control what happened. In his room he was safe.

People stared at him out here as well. They looked at his cane and he knew what was going through their minds.

Why does he have a cane when he's so young?

What's wrong with him?

Is he a freak?

"I want to go back," Mike said tersely, twisting around, feeling a need to get back to the car. Michelle grabbed his arm though and held him back.

"Come on Mike, we're only going to be a little while. Maybe there's something in there that you'd like as well, a little treat?"

Mike remembered her using the same trick to get him to go in there when he was younger. How easily children were bought. It wasn't going to work this time. He shook his head firmly.

"They're all staring at me. They all think I'm a freak," he mumbled, casting a wary glare around the parking lot.

"Nobody thinks that," Michelle said. "And even if they do, it's their own problem. They don't know what a brave man you are."

"I'm not brave. I just got lucky," Mike said.

Michelle stepped closer to him and lowered her voice to a whisper. The words rushed out of her mouth like a torrent of wind. "I prayed every day for you to come back to me and here you are. I know it's not fair and that you lost people you cared about, but the fact is that you're here and I'm not going to be upset about that. Please Mike, just come in with me. Try and do something normal for once. It's the only way you're going to get used to being back here."

Mike bit his tongue to stop himself from saying something he was going to regret. Why couldn't she understand that all he wanted was to stay in his room where is quiet and safe and he didn't have to put himself into these awkward situations? Why didn't she understand that there was no reason for him to have survived while people like Aaron died? It was all pointless. But at the same time, he depended on her. Without his parents he would have been cast out onto the streets, becoming one of the forgotten people. He shouldn't resent her for that, and yet he was filled with turbulent emotions because he hated the idea that he should be as dependent on her now as he was as a child. She and his father didn't deserve that either.

He hung his head as he walked in beside her, trying to keep his head low, even though he could feel the stares of all the people around him. They burned, and in his mind the air shimmered and crackled with fire. He heard the explosion again. The chattering voices receded into the distance and transformed into machine gun fire. Then there was smoke and suddenly he was running for his life. And then pain. Something ached in his stomach. He winced and pressed his hand to his gut. The scar had healed over, but the pain still remained. When he took his hand away, he expected it to be covered in blood, but his palm was clear. Anxious sweat stung his eyes.

"Mike? Mike?" he heard his mother call. She had a worried look on her face.

"I'm sorry Mom," he mumbled, turning his face away as he saw that other people had gathered around him and were looking at him with intrigue, like he was some kind of victim. "I need to get out of here." He pushed past her and this time he wasn't going to listen to any of her arguments. The noises were all so loud and he wondered how anyone could stand being locked in that cacophony. He breathed a sigh of relief as he burst out into the free, fresh air of the parking lot. He hobbled to the car and leaned against the hood, staring up at the night sky. It reminded him of a night long ago before all this happened, a night when he was yet to become a man, when he was with his best friend. But like everything else that had come to an end, and that night was more like a dream now.

Michelle returned shortly with a bag full of shopping. "I went as quickly as I could. I only got the essentials. Are you all right?"

Mike nodded. "I just needed to get out of there. It was so noisy. It reminded me of... of back there."

Michelle had a look of concern on her face. "I know that we've spoken about it before, but are you sure you don't want to speak to someone? I think it would help you."

"No," he snapped, and then immediately softened. "No," he repeated, holding out his palm. "I just want to be left alone in my room where it's safe. I just need time to adjust, that's all," he said, and pulled the door open. Michelle had a worried look on her face, but she said nothing more.

When they returned home, Mike went straight to his room and fell into bed. The relief was palpable. This place was his safe haven and he didn't have to worry about anything here. There were no expectations and no demands on his time. He could just look at the TV and lose himself in the flashing images. There was always something to watch, always something to distract his mind. The door swung open and his father stepped in. Hank was a tall, broad shouldered man, still retaining the vigor and strength of his youth.

"Your mom told me what happened this evening. Do you want to talk about anything?" he asked.

"No," Mike replied.

Hank sighed and leaned against the door frame. "You know, the world has changed a lot since I was young. Back then the idea of being a man was that you took everything on the chin and never complained, never showed any weakness, because then the enemy knew they were getting to you. But I've seen too many of my friends struggle with anger issues and depression and all kinds of other things because they wouldn't talk about their problems." He moved further into the room and perched himself on the end of Mike's bed, lowering his voice. "I haven't told you this before, but if I hadn't learned to be open with my emotions then I probably wouldn't be here now. Your mom and I, we… we had our problems and I didn't want to deal with them because I thought if I ignored them, they would all just go away. But that's the thing; they don't. They just get worse and worse, but you don't have to go through this alone son. Your mom taught me how to express myself and how to communicate with her and it saved our marriage. I know it sounds hokey and it's not easy at first, but we can both see that you're struggling with something and we just want you to know that you can talk to us. You're not alone. You never will be as long as we're around."

He waited for Mike to say something, but Mike didn't have anything to offer. Hank nodded and sighed, and then left Mike to his own devices. Mike knew that it was in his best interests to talk, but he didn't know where to begin. There were so many thoughts raging around his mind that it was almost too much to bear. Instead, he stayed in his room, quietly, losing himself in his TV shows.

He was but a shadow of his former self and it was easier for everyone if he was allowed to stay in the depths of his room, in this cavern of solitude he had created for himself. He couldn't fathom talking to anyone about his problems or seeing anyone from his past. He hated the thought of them seeing how he had changed, the monster he had become. It was better that he was forgotten. It would have been better had he died out there and was laid to rest with Aaron.

Chapter Four

Jim pulled up outside Mike's house. He had driven by it often over the years, but it had been a long time since he had ever been inside. It used to be a second home to him, and little had changed. The lawn was still trimmed neatly, and the front yard was filled with clusters of colorful flowers. Nerves swam in his stomach, which he thought was stupid because he and Mike had spent so much time over the years, he shouldn't have been nervous at all. And yet this wasn't the Mike that he knew. This was a Mike who had been to war, who had seen all kinds of horrors, and who had returned injured. Jim didn't even know if Mike would want to see him.

He cleared his throat and swallowed his nerves, rubbing his clammy palms on his top as he walked up the front yard. Part of his anxiety came from the fact that he had lied to Ryan as well. He wasn't even sure why he had lied, but didn't Ryan deserve to know that Mike had been more than a friend to him? Or at least Jim had thought of him as more than a friend. Those feelings were a long time in the past though, ancient history. There was no place for them now.

Jim glanced up at the tree that brushed against the window of Mike's room. He remembered scampering up it and climbing into the window when he should have been sleeping. A smile played upon his face at the misadventures they used to get up to, and he couldn't help but wonder what his life would have been like had Mike not left for the army. There was a lump in his throat as he thought about all the memories that would have been made…would he have managed to come clean about his feelings to Mike?

In an instant another life flashed in his mind, as though a lightning bolt had illuminated a murky night sky.

***

Everything would have gone differently. Instead of Mike confessing something to him, Jim would have confessed something to Mike. In stammering, stumbling words Jim would have told Mike how he felt, peeling back the layers of his heart, smashing through the emotional wall he had spent so long constructing. The words would have poured out of him and he knew he wouldn't be able to look at Mike until he spoke.

"Oh Jim…" Mike would have said in that ever so calm way he always said things, as though everything had always been all right and would forever be all right between them, for no storm could ever capsize their friendship. He would have reached out and touched Jim on the hand, a touch so innocent and yet so laced with danger. "I'm so flattered and I, well, I guess I've been waiting for you to say something like this. I thought there was something there, but I just wasn't sure," he would have said.

Jim would have laughed lightly, as though it was all just some silly misunderstanding. But then he would have looked into Mike's eyes, falling into those stormy irises with all the abandon of a plummeting comet. The hand was still there, the touch heavy upon in. With every moment that passed it seemed as though their flesh melted into each other, becoming closer with one another.

Mike would have told Jim that he had signed up to join the army. Instead of pleading with Mike on rational grounds, Jim would have tried to tether him with emotion.

"You can't leave me Mike. I love you. Please, don't leave me alone. Don't go all the way out there where you might never come back. Think of the life we can have together. I know you find it difficult to fit in, but you can fit in with me. We've only ever needed each other. We can find our place in the world, together."

His words would have been laced with emotion, his voice cracking like a tumultuous wave. And Mike would have replied simply, as he always did.

"Okay," he would have said. "I won't leave you because I love you as well Jim." And then he would have leaned in and scorched Jim with his lips. Jim would have twisted and melted from the inside out, and the world would have taken on a new color, as though he had never really seen things properly before.

There would have been celebration as they came out as a couple, two lives becoming one and it would have felt so right.

"We always knew there was something between you," people would say. Jim and Mike would laugh. They'd date for an endless summer and lose themselves in hazy dreams and long nights and creaking beds, and eventually they would find a place of their own. It was a modern fairytale and the only ending would be a happy one because they would be together, forever, and nothing could tear them apart.

***

But life hadn't turned out like that. Jim hadn't confessed his feelings and Mike had gone to war. There was a lump in Jim's throat as he walked up to the door. He held his hand before he knocked, thinking of Ryan, dear sweet Ryan who had shown him the ways of romance and swept away the fog of uncertainty that had always clouded Jim's view. A pang of guilt nestled in his heart even though he knew he had every right to be here, but it still felt wrong, because he hadn't told Ryan the truth about his past feelings for Mike.

But did they even need to be spoke about? The feelings were a thing of the past. They only existed now as a whisper in the back of Jim's soul.

The door opened almost immediately.

"Jim!" Michelle said excitedly. Jim could tell that she had been through the wringer. He remembered her as a porcelain doll, never a hair out of place or wrinkles on her clothes, with immaculate makeup accentuating her natural beauty. But here she looked lost. There was a certain look in her eyes, a look that touched his heart. He could see the shadows under her eyes and the small wrinkles on her lips where she had gnawed at them like a beaver. "It's been so long and it's so good to see you!" She opened her arms to him and embraced him like a long-lost friend. Suddenly Jim was surrounded in a cloud of sweet perfume and he was taken back to a time when it drifted into Mike's room on stolen nights. They joked that they would always be able to smell her coming, and so never had to worry about being caught when they stayed up longer than they should.

"Yeah, it has," Jim replied.

Michelle rolled back on her heels and regarded him with a look of wonder. "You've grown up into a handsome young man. How are you doing? How are your folks?"

"Oh yeah we're all great," Jim replied with a smile. "How are you?"

"You know, getting by," she said, forcing a smile to appear on her face. The muscles didn't seem as though they wanted to move. Jim could sense the strained emotion under her words.

"I heard that Mike was back and I wanted to come by and say hi."

"That's wonderful. Really it's…" she pressed a hand to her mouth and closed her eyes, composing herself against swelling emotion. "He could really use a friend right now."

"Yeah, it's been too long. How is he?"

"He's… he's having a hard time adjusting to it all. You know how it is," Michelle said. Jim nodded, but he didn't know how it was at all. She welcomed him in an offered him a drink. He didn't know how she did it, but she always made lemonade taste magical. He sipped from the glass and nodded to Hank, who smiled, but looked lost, as though he had something else on his mind. Memories flooded back as Jim walked through this house that had once been so familiar to him. But there was something that had changed about it as well, some kind of sorrow that hung over the place like a cloud. Hank and Michelle had always seemed like the epitome of the American Dream. He had been the quarterback, she had been the cheerleader, and their sweetheart romance had blossomed into a lasting marriage. But now there was a chink in that image, a crack that threatened to shatter it all apart, and Jim was about to meet the source.

He wasn't sure what was going to wait for him when he went into Mike's room. The door was ajar. It creaked slightly as he pushed it open. The curtains had been drawn and the room was illuminated by the flashing images of the TV screen, false moonlight that flickered and danced, but that could be dispelled in an instant. It was like going back in time. The posters that hung on the wall were the same, as were the books that were sitting on shelves. Nothing had changed at all in the room apart from the man, the man had changed.

When Jim's gaze drifted toward Mike, he almost gasped. Mike was sitting there in bed, his feet up, a cane leaning against the wall next to him. His hair was tousled, his jaws covered with a shadow of stubble. A dirty t-shirt with holes in it adorned his glorious body, and pajama pants were visible underneath the bed covers. Mike had a surly look on his face and for a moment Jim could have sworn the man was a statue as his eyes were transfixed by the screen.

"Mike?" Jim ventured. It happened slowly, but the golem head turned and an empty stare fell upon him. Jim wasn't quite prepared for the way Mike would look at him, with this emptiness in his eyes, as though he was looking through Jim, not at him. It was in that moment Jim realized his best friend had not returned complete.

"Hey," Mike said, without emotion, utterly neutral, as though this was simply one of those moments in life that passed by without a second thought. Jim moved further into the room without permission. He pulled a chair out from the desk and perched in it, turning his back toward the TV. Mike seemed to be trying not to look at him.

"What do you mean 'hey'? Come on Mike, it's me… it's Jim! Say something. It's been so long."

Mike turned to him. "Hey," he replied. Jim was crestfallen. He hadn't known what to expect when he saw Mike like this. Perhaps there would have been fireworks. Perhaps there would have been a moment where Mike awoke from this slumber and all his emotions would have poured out in a torrent. Perhaps he would have said how he had made a mistake in leaving and that the only thing that kept him going in the Middle East was the thought of coming home to Jim.

But he didn't say any of those things.

"I heard from Mom that you were back. I'm a little surprise that I didn't hear it from you."

"I wasn't sure if you'd want to see me."

"Why would I not want to see you?" Jim asked, confused. "I'm sorry we lost touch over the years…"

"It wasn't your fault. Things were sketchy over there," Mike said. Then he caught Jim looking at his legs. The next words that came from his mouth weren't devoid of emotion at all. They were laced with something sharp, something deadly. "Take a guess," he said.

"What?" Jim mumbled.

"You're wondering which one is the one that hurts, right? Well go on, take a guess. You have a fifty-fifty chance." There was almost something mocking about Mike's tone, and Jim certainly wasn't going to play such a morbid game.

"I wasn't-" Jim began, but Mike cut him off.

"Everyone does. It's only natural. It's this one, if you must know," he said, lifting the wounded leg a few inches off the ground."

"I wouldn't have been able to tell."

"I can," Mike replied. He leaned his head back and looked up at the ceiling.

"So… how are you finding it being home?" Jim ventured, wishing that they could broach all the years that had passed and go back to speaking about everything and nothing. There was a chasm that had opened between them and Jim wasn't sure if it was possible to travel over it.

"Oh it's just fine, you know, everyone treats me like a hero, I get to do whatever I like. I mean, yeah, I always dreamed about living with my parents and being a cripple."

"You're not a cripple Mike," Jim said. Mike just glared at him.

"I'm not, *not* a cripple either," he said quietly.

"I missed you," Jim said, hoping that it might pull Mike back away from this grim outlook. "I want to hear everything that's happened to you over the years."

"Are you sure you can handle that?" Mike asked. "It's not exactly a story with a happy ending."

"The story isn't over yet Mike. You still have plenty to live," Jim said.

Mike merely grunted. "It's not worth living."

"Mike, surely you don't mean that? Come on, this isn't like you."

"What's 'like me'?" he suddenly thundered. "It's been four years Jim. I'm not the same guy you used to know. Things have changed and I'm never going to be that guy again, so you might as well leave now. The friend that you knew doesn't exist anymore. Just go and return to whatever life you've built for yourself. I'm sure it's great and I'm happy for you, but I don't need your pity to get me through the days. I'm doing just fine on my own," he said, and immediately grabbed the remote control to increase the volume on the TV. Jim sat there open mouthed. Part of him wanted to argue with Mike and tell him how crazy he was being, but another part was so shocked that he just wanted to crawl away and do as Mike commanded.

"I just thought we could catch up..." Jim said, but his words were drowned out by the TV. Mike clenched his jaw tightly and didn't take his eyes off the TV. The chair creaked as Jim rose and he left the room with an ache in his heart.

Whoever that man was in there, he wasn't Jim's friend.

***

Jim staggered down the stairs, his footsteps heavy and laden with guilt. Michelle hopped out from the lounge and glanced at Jim with hope in her eyes. Suddenly Jim understood the sorrow that had taken its toll on her. Suddenly he knew the burden that had been placed upon her. In just one conversation Mike had cut him down, slashing his efforts to reach him with a scythe. How painful must it have been for his mother to be pushed away like that?

"That was quick," she said with a hint of anxiety in her voice.

"Yeah. I don't think he was really in the mood for visitors," Jim said. Michelle looked crestfallen. It was as though she was a puppet and one the strings that held her up had just been cut. Her entire body slumped in one motion.

"Oh," she said, sighing heavily. "I thought a visit from an old friend would have cheered him up. I thought…" she trailed away for a moment and looked as lost as her son, but then her gaze flicked up. "I'm sorry that you wasted your time. Thank you for coming by anyway," she offered, showing him to the door.

It would have been so easy for Jim to leave then, but he couldn't bring himself to be so cruel. The bonds of friendship that had been forged in their youth had not eroded yet. Jim placed his hand against the frame of the door. "What happened to him?"

"There was an accident. He was caught in the crossfire. He saw his friends die and then he was sent back here. That's what I know from what the reports say, but he won't tell me what really happened. He won't talk about any of it. I don't know if he's upset because of what happened or because he's not over there anymore. I just don't know. He just sits in his room losing himself. It's like another piece of him disappears every day and all I want is for him to come back to me. All I want is my son to come back to me and I don't know if he ever will." The words turned into sobs and crystal tears trickled down her cheeks. She wiped them away immediately, as though she was apologizing for them or ashamed of them.

"Has he spoke to anyone about it?"

She shook her head. "He won't. That's why I was so glad to see you. I thought that maybe he would open up. I keep telling myself that he just needs time, but he doesn't have all the time in the world. The longer he waits the harder it's going to be and this… this isn't the life I wanted for him Jim. I just wanted him to be happy."

"I know," Jim said. "Look, if there's anything I can do to help just let me know. I don't like the thought of him being alone like this."

Jim reached out and touched Michelle lightly on the shoulder. She nodded as relief shone on her face. "You're a sweet boy Jim. He was always lucky to have a friend like you."

"No," Jim smiled. "I was lucky to have a friend like him."

***

"So how was the soldier boy?" Ryan asked when Jim returned home. The apartment smelled clean. Ryan was wearing a tight t shirt and slacks. He'd been unpacking more things, making the place their own. Jim sighed and slouched on the couch, rubbing his temples.

"Not great. He was so... lost. That's the only way I can describe him. I was in the same room as him but it was like he wasn't there. He gave me the impression that he wanted to be anywhere else. And his mom, oh, she's been through a lot. She told me that he doesn't talk about what happened to him and that all he does is stay in his room."

"That's horrible. And people wonder why I hate war," Ryan said with a shake of the head. "It's all fine to celebrate the glory of fighting, but when the war is over people just move on. It's not right."

"No, it's not," Jim said.

"I guess not everyone can be helped though. Hopefully, he'll be able to open up in time and get the help he needs."

"I think I need to help him," Jim said.

"Jim, you're not a counselor."

"No, but I am his friend and I can't take seeing him like this. I can't just let him wither."

For a moment Jim thought that this was going to break out into an argument, but instead Ryan sat beside him and kissed him on the forehead. "You are a good man, a far better man that I deserve," he said. "Now let me run you a bath. It sounds like you could use something to relax."

Jim smiled in anticipation of the warm suds caressing his long body. But Ryan's words rattled around his mind. Perhaps it was he who didn't deserve Ryan. Was it so impossible to tell him that once upon a time he was in love with this man he was so determined to help? But what Pandora's Box would be opened if he did?

Chapter Five

The water came down in a slashing torrent. Aside from being in his bed in front of the TV, the shower was Mike's favorite place to be as it was the only place where the world was drowned out. Steam rose around him like a fine mist, and the water peppered his body with a reminder that he was alive. The heat was blistering and his leg trembled whenever he put any weight on it, so he had to steady himself by placing a palm flat against the tiled wall. Lank hair straggled across his scalp and his mouth hung open. The water cascaded down, some slipping into his open mouth, the warmth settling on his tongue. He closed his eyes as he pushed his face into the water, wishing that somehow it would wash away all the pain inside him and send it careening down into the sewers.

Seeing Jim again had shocked him. Here was a link to his past that shamed him. How was he supposed to let Jim see what a wreck he had become? Jim looked good though. Life had been kind to him and Mike was at least glad that it had been kind to one of them. He knew he had been bitter, but he couldn't help lashing out. It was an instinctive reaction now. Jim had better things to do with his time anyway. Better that he be driven away now so that he didn't have to waste his time with Mike. After Jim had left, Mike had crept to the door and listened to the murmured conversation. He heard what his mother had said to Jim, and the words pained him. It wasn't as though he wanted to be different, he just was, and he didn't know how to change it. What was the point of dredging up the horrible memories? All he wanted to do was escape the world and live in this cocoon. Was that so bad? Why did people always push and harry others to live in this community when sometimes all people needed was to be left alone.

Anger flared inside him as Mike slammed his fist against the wall. Water sprayed out and he started weeping. He didn't know where the tears came from, but suddenly they were flowing down his cheeks, mixing in with the water from the shower until the two were indistinguishable. Then he turned the faucet and there was silence, deathly, suffocating silence. Drying himself, he staggered back to his room and fell into bed.

"At least he's showering," he heard his father say.

The night was sleepless, as all the others were. Whenever Mike closed his eyes he was taken back to that tragic moment where everything had changed. Perhaps he was different. That moment had been his new birth, his baptism. Whenever he thought back to a time before that it all just seemed hollow, like a shadow of a memory that was more akin to a dream. When he thought about the time he and Jim had spent together in those halcyon days when wasting time at school was their biggest problem, it seemed unreal. He couldn't believe that that had been him and that he had been preoccupied with those petty concerns. And then there was Jim. There were times when it had been so painful to be around him, every moment fraught with tension. Their friendship had been the most precious thing to him and he had never dared do anything to jeopardize it. But now that had been lost to him as well. Back when he had joined the army the only thing that held him back was the thought of not being around Jim again. In fact, there had been a part of him that had been tempted to stay when Jim had begged him not to go, but he was stubborn and foolhardy. It was difficult to say what would have happened had Jim remained at home. Perhaps things would have been better, but then there would have been no Aaron either. His love and companionship had been the only softness Mike had found in the desert. Amid all the scratchy, dusty heat, Aaron had been an oasis.

Oh, fate was certainly a trickster. The winding, twisting corridors of a life were always explored with eagerness and the ones that seemed to hold the brightest hope were often a trap. There was always too much to give up, a sacrifice that couldn't be made. Mike couldn't very well reach into his heart and tear out all the sorrow because, in some way, those were the parts that made him most human. But they also prevented him from moving on. He knew that he was frozen in time. He could feel the world slipping away from him, but he didn't know how to stop it. He knew that one day too his parents would get tired of supporting this hollow husk of a man that used to be their son, and they wondered when they would begin seeing him as the stranger he truly was.

Then, he would truly be doomed.

But all he wanted was to be left alone. One day he knew that he was going to get his wish, and even though he knew it was going to be the most terrible day of his life he could not stop himself from wanting it.

***

The sun was bright outside, but Mike only had a faint hint at it through the curtains as he kept them drawn, wanting to shut the rest of the world away. If he kept it at arm's length then it couldn't hurt him. Life was pain and the only way to stop himself from feeling all this darkness and sorrow was to hide himself away and lose himself in fiction. TV was easy and comforting. Life was pain. He had made so many sacrifices already, so one more didn't make a difference. Sure, if he really tried, he might be able to reconnect with others and have some semblance of a normal life, or at least the appearance of one. He could certainly fool others and he might even be able to fool himself for a time, but in the end, he would always know he was an imposter. There had been a mistake in the cosmic thread of the world. He should have died along with Aaron. He should have been spared this misery because all the goodness in the world didn't make up for the pain residing in his stomach.

"Hey, I thought we could take a walk."

Mike had been so lost in his own mind that he hadn't realized Jim was standing there.

"What are you doing back here?"

"I'm asking you to come hang out," Jim said.

"I already told you that I don't need your pity Jim," he spat, "and it's not like you want to go for a walk with me anyway. I can't exactly go very far."

"I just thought we could go to the park like we used to and sit around and people watch. It's a beautiful day out there. It's gotta be better than sitting in here and watching TV all day. There's only so much of that you can do before you lose your mind."

"Thanks for the offer, but I'll pass. I know that Mom must have put you up to this. You don't have to bow down to her pressure and you don't have to feel guilty about walking away. I never asked you to help me."

"That's the thing about friends Mike, you don't have to ask them to help. I'm not here because of your mom. I'm here because I want to be here. I'm here because I've missed you and I want to catch up. God, has it really been long enough that you've forgotten about our friendship?"

"It's been a lifetime," Mike said quietly. Anger and caution danced within him, like two flames fighting with each other, creating an inferno inside him. All Mike wanted to do was push Jim away.

"Four years isn't a lifetime Mike. Come on, it'll be fun." When Mike didn't answer, Jim's tone became sterner. "I'm your friend and I'm going to let you waste away your days here. You're not alone Mike. We either hang out here or we can hang out outside. Either way I'm not leaving until we've spent a few good hours together, and frankly the way this place smells I'd rather go outside where there's some fresh air. It almost smells as bad as that time we stayed here and did that *Star Trek* marathon."

Something in the back of Mike's mind flickered and he couldn't stop the smile from appearing on his face. "It got worse after we took that break to go and throw a Frisbee around."

"Yeah, I never got why we didn't stop to have a shower before we started watching them again," Jim said, smiling. Mike chuckled a little at the memory, but he was almost afraid of it taking hold in his mind.

"I'm not the same as I used to be Jim."

"I know, and that's okay. I'm not the same as I used to be either. It'll be fun seeing how different we are. Come on, at least just for a few hours," he said. Mike glanced at the narrow opening of sunlight, and couldn't deny that he would appreciate a change of scenery. It was clear that Jim had this crusade in mind as well, and he wasn't going to be deterred. No matter, Mike thought, after spending a few hours in misery with him, Jim would realize that there was no saving him and he'd give up this act of charity once and for all.

***

Mike couldn't help but notice the quiet surprise on his mother's face when he left with Jim. She was proud of him, as though he was a toddler going to nursery without crying. Pitiful. Pathetic. He was a grown man, but in so many ways he was still just like a child. A scowl appeared on his face as he hobbled out toward Jim's car. In the past they would have run to park, but now they drove across the smooth roads and pulled up in the parking spots. The park was a wide open area, a lagoon of beauty amid the city that had risen around it. Paths spread out in all directions in meandering ways. In the distance Mike could hear the sound of people playing football. A gleaming Frisbee soared through the sapphire sky. The vivid color of the grass made it seem as though he had stepped into another world, one drenched with the permanent promise of youth.

He walked alongside Jim as they made their way to a rising slope that was shaded by trees. It looked out over a large lake. A few people were sitting by the edge, letting their feet hang into cold water. Others stood by, tossing bread and seeds to ducks. Mike smiled as he saw the ducks pluck the bread out of the air with their beaks and then shake their heads. The giggles of amused children drifted toward them on the calm air.

"See, this isn't so bad, is it?" Jim said.

The words immediately dispelled the comfortable feeling. "What do you really want Jim?"

"I told you that I wanted to catch up. Four years is a long time and I thought it would be fun to know what's happened in our lives. I mean, you were the only person who helped me get through my teenage years. I don't know what I would have done without you."

"Seems like you've been doing all right without me so far," Mike shot back. Jim turned away from him and tore up a few blades of grass, ripping them between his fingers.

"You know what I mean Mike. We were good friends. Best friends. I don't like seeing you like this. I just want things to go back to the way they were."

"They can't Jim. That's just a fact of life. I know you probably came here thinking that things were going to be the same, but they're not. I'm not the same guy that you knew," Mike said. Part of him wanted to be, but he knew that it wasn't possible.

"I know that Mike I just..." Jim grunted in frustration and looked to the sky. "I just hate thinking that you're back here and we're not friends. It seems wrong. I know that we've had a lot of time apart, but through it all there have been moments when I wanted to share things with you or laugh about things with you, or a movie has started playing that I wanted to see with you. It might have been four years, but I never forgot our friendship." He turned to look at Mike. "Did you?"

"No, I didn't."

"Good. Then let's at least try and pick up from where we left off. I didn't spend all that time with you in school to end up being strangers," Jim said, wearing a wry smile. Mike didn't laugh.

"I'm not going to talk about what happened if that's what you're hoping. And you're not going to be able to talk me into seeing a counselor."

Jim held up his hands. "I never said any of that. I just want to hang out."

"Yeah, but I know that's what my mom wants. How about you talk and I'll listen. What's been happening with you?"

"Well, I mean, college was pretty hectic and it wasn't like I thought it would be. I mean, I figured I'd be more popular and that it would be different from school, but it was the same. There were so many cliques and I really wish you had been there so it would have been easier. I didn't really have anyone to make fun of everyone else with. Anyway, that did have the benefit of giving me a lot of time to study. So, I hunkered down and did the best I could. Ended up getting pretty good grades and then I applied for a government job overseeing the animal welfare services. The pay is good and I get to feel like I'm doing something good with my time. It's not exactly what I always dreamed of, but it's a decent living and I'm happy." He paused for a moment, and when he spoke again there was something different about his voice, something wary. "I also just moved in with my boyfriend. He's name is Ryan."

"That's... that's great," Mike said, not entirely sure what to do with this information. "It sounds like you've really landed on your feet. I'm happy that life has been so kind to you."

"Yeah, but I still... I don't know. Part of me wishes that things could have been different."

"In what way?"

"You know in what way. I wish that you had never left. The world might have been kind to me, but it would have been more fun if you had still been around."

"I had a job to do," Mike replied.

"I know you thought it was your duty but I just… oh I don't know what I'm saying." Jim turned his gaze to the lake. Mike looked forward too and all the hours they had whiled away together seemed like wasted time now.

"I'm sorry Jim. I'm sorry that I couldn't be the friend that you needed."

"Hey, that's not what I was saying. I'm not trying to make you feel guilty for this. I just want to try and connect with you."

"Why?" Mike asked, the level of his voice rising so that it broke the idyllic stillness of the day. "Why are you so intent on this Jim? You seem to have a pretty sweet life for yourself, and I can't imagine your boyfriend is too happy about you spending time with some broken soldier. Maybe it's better if you just stick to what you know and mind your own business. We can't recapture our youth. Maybe it's better that we just leave things be."

Mike pushed himself up, using his cane as leverage. The ground was uneven and he cursed his leg yet again for not doing what he wanted it to do. He strained to use the cane and he trembled with anger. This was a mistake. He should never have done this. All he needed was to return home where he could be safe, where he could trust that nothing would hurt him.

Chapter Six

Jim was aghast when he saw Mike hobble away. Mike had never been one to let his temper get the best of him, but now it flared up and his eyes were filled with a storm. Jim scrambled up and ran after Mike.

"Don't just walk away Mike. That's not like you," he said, reaching out to tug at Mike's arm. It didn't take Jim long to catch up with him as he could easily walk at a quicker pace. Mentioning Ryan had filled him with guilt, even though it shouldn't have. It's not as though his love for Mike still existed... did it?

Mike shrugged off Jim's touch, still surprisingly strong. "How many times do I have to tell you? I'm not the guy you knew! I've changed Jim. You have to let go of this version you have of me," he spat.

"You keep saying that, but I know it's still you in there Mike. I'm not willing to give up on all our years of friendship. For God's sake why won't you just talk to me? I know it's been a long time, but you can't keep hiding from your problems. You can't just stay in your room all the time. That definitely isn't you and the people who care about you the most know it. Are we all wrong? Are you that arrogant to say that we're the ones who are in the wrong here?" Jim's words flew from his mouth like arrows, and he couldn't hold back his emotion any longer. It felt as though his friend's life was in the balance and he couldn't dare let Mike walk away without telling him what was really on his mind.

"I want to help you Mike, and it's not because I pity you or because I feel sorry for you or because I feel guilty. It's just for the pure and simple reason that I care about you. I know you've been gone for a long time, but have you really forgotten what it's like to have someone care about you? Were those four years so lonely that you had nobody to count on? Nobody that was looking out for you?"

Mike suddenly stopped and placed both hands on the head of this cane. He bowed his head.

"I had someone. His name was Aaron. He looked out for me. He made the whole place better. And then he died." He looked up and gazed directly at Jim, his eyes so wide that Jim could see the whites of them clearly. "He died and I lived and I had to watch it happen. I saw the moment when his life just went," he snapped his fingers, "so yeah, I had someone to watch out for me, but he didn't have anyone to watch out for him. I was supposed to keep him safe Jim, but I couldn't, so maybe it's for your own sake that you keep your distance for me because people who get close get hurt, and you clearly have plenty going on in your life that you don't need that kind of trouble, so just take me back home and leave me alone. I don't want this. I don't need this. I just want to be left alone."

There was a mournful, whimpering quality to his voice that tugged at Jim's heart strings. Jim listened to what he said intently and he suddenly realized why Mike had been pushing everyone away. Jim rushed up to Mike and wrapped his arms around him in a tight hug, as though he was telling Mike with his body that he was never going to let him go. Mike resisted at first, but then the cane dropped and his arms clung to Jim. He trembled. Jim could feel the quaking body and all the sorrow that tainted him.

"It's not your fault," Jim said, over and over again. "It's not your fault."

***

They were sitting in a small café that overlooked a wide expanse of the park. There was a running track that was currently empty, and in the distance, there were people bouncing on trampolines. Mike and Jim sat with their orange sodas in front of them, the shade of the café protecting them from the glare of the sun. They had two tubs of ice cream as well, rich and delicious dessert that helped to take the edge off the fraught emotion.

"So, will you tell me about him?" Jim asked. Never in a million years had he expected to be asking about a man who had captured Mike's heart. He had always expected envy to flare up inside him. Somehow it seemed as though he and Mike had been meant to share their first forays into love together, to feel the blossoming spring of arousal seize their bodies drift into the unexplored mist, discovering the wonders together. Even now there was a spike of remorse that they had broken vows that had never been made, but Jim pushed these thoughts aside.

Mike scooped up a large dollop of dark ice cream and slid it between his lips. He spoke quietly, but at least he spoke.

"We met when we were first deployed. God, I was so nervous," he laughed a little. "I know it seemed like it was something I always wanted to do, but when I got out there, I was wondering if I had made a mistake. Part of me just wanted to turn around and come back home and pretend that it had all been some kind of prank, but there were too many stern faces looking at me to do that. We fell into our platoon and I just so happened to share a bunk with Aaron. We fell into a pretty good rhythm and he had such a stupid sense of humor. He reminded me of you in that respect," Mike smiled. Jim laughed too. "We started having a laugh together and making up jokes. It was really the only way we could make it out there. There were other people who were serious and never cracked a smile, and I don't know how they did it. If I didn't laugh so much, I would have lost my mind. We talked about whatever came to mind, and sometimes we'd sit up at night and look at the stars, wondering what the people at home were doing. It was weird you know, they were the same stars that you were looking at, and yet we were in another world. One night we were sitting there in silence and the next thing I knew we were holding hands. It felt strange and yet it felt right as well."

Jim was jealous of Aaron because he had the courage to make a move. There had been so many times when he had longed to take Mike's hand, but he had always hesitated. Aaron hadn't showed such uncertainty, and he had reaped the rewards.

"We were partners in crime and we were able to share our deepest emotions and fears with each other. Some nights were so scary. We saw people being brought back. We heard their screams and we knew one day that it could be us. We had this thing where we asked ourselves every day why we were still out there, and we promised ourselves that if we ever couldn't answer that question then we would give up and ship home. I spoke a lot about you and how you had been the only person to help me get through school. He spoke about his family and friend as well, and when we did this it felt like we were a little closer to home."

Jim watched emotions play upon Mike's face. He could see how difficult it was to relive these memories, and he appreciated how Mike was finally opening up to him.

"It came time for our tour to end and we both knew that if we went home, we weren't sure if we could still be together. It required one of us to uproot and travel to the other side of the country, so it seemed more natural to stay out there where we were used to everything. We signed up again and everything continued just like it was. We had this perfect life in this imperfect place and then it all went to hell."

Jim noticed that Mike's hand trembled. He hadn't taken another scoop of ice cream in all the time he had been talking about Aaron, so it had melted into this dark ooze. Mike had that look again, as though he was peering beyond the veil of reality to somewhere different.

"What happened?" Jim asked gently, his words as soft as the wind. For a moment he thought that Mike was going to erupt with anger at him again and he would storm away, but that wasn't the case this time. Instead, Mike leaned down to look at his open palms and sighed heavily.

"We were on a routine mission to defuse a bomb, but then the air became alive with bullets. People shouted at us and our truck got hit. We scrambled out. It was an ambush. We tried to make our way to safety, but then Aaron he... he got hit. It was over in an instant and he... he saved me. I couldn't believe it when I saw what had happened. He just slumped to the floor and we'd just been joking about what movie we were going to watch. It all ended in an instant and that was it Jim. That was it. It was just so quick, something so precious was destroyed and I had nothing left. I woke up in a hospital with them telling me that I was being shipped home. I didn't have any say in the matter. I didn't get to go to his funeral. I didn't get to say goodbye. I was just taken and told to get on with life, but I can't. I can't, not without him. I shouldn't be here Jim. He deserves to live, not me."

Jim digested the harrowing tale and felt a mixture of emotions within his heart. His throat dried, and no amount of soda would quench this thirst. Mike leaned his head against his hands. His shoulders shook with sorrow. Jim reached out to hold out his hand.

"Hey, Mike, it's okay. Hey. It's okay. I know this is hard-"

"You don't know," Mike snapped.

"Okay, so I don't know. But what I do know is that you're still here and that has to mean something. I don't know how the world works and who deserves what, but the fact is that you're here and you have to ask yourself if Aaron would want you living like this?"

"Oh, I've asked myself that plenty of times but the point is that he isn't here, isn't it? I don't get to ask him and I don't get to know what it would be like if he was still here. I just have the memories of him, and every day they seem to get a little farther away."

"That's because you keep running from them Mike. You need to talk to your parents about this. They're worried about you. If you told them about Aaron they'd understand more, and it would help give him life as well. By talking about him and sharing your memories of him you're keeping him alive. I know it's painful, but it's a good thing. I wish I had the chance to meet him."

"Yeah, I think you would have liked him."

"I'm sure I would have. Thank you for telling me about him," Jim said sincerely. Mike looked up at him and suddenly their eyes met. Jim was awhirl with emotion as he gazed into those fathomless eyes. All at once he saw the person Mike used to be, but also saw the man he was, a man haunted with pain. More than that, he saw beauty.

"I'm sorry," Mike said.

"You don't have to be sorry for anything," Jim reassured him.

"No, I do. I've been a jerk when you've just been trying to help me it's just that I've been away for so long and war does something to you... I'm not sure I'll ever be the same again."

"But that's okay too Mike. Life is about change. None of us are the same. We just have to adapt with the changes and trust that there are people who care about us and want the best for us. I'm here for you Mike and I'm not going anywhere."

Mike pressed his lips together firmly and smiled. He nodded a little and then sniffed back his sorrow. He swirled his spoon around the puddle that had been his ice cream and pushed it aside.

"Tell me about Ryan," he said.

Jim wondered where he was going to be begin.

Chapter Seven

Mike had to admit that he felt better after seeing Jim. Jim always had a way of getting him to talk about things that he found uncomfortable. It actually surprised him that things had largely remained the same between them despite all the years that had passed. The initial awkwardness that followed their reunion had completely vanished, and by the time they were ready to leave the park it was as though no time had passed at all.

And yet it was impossible to forget that so much had changed, for both of them. Mike had gone off to war, fallen in love, and then lost the man he had given his heart to. A little piece of his heart had been left behind as well. As for Jim, well, he had made something of himself. He was happy, standing a little taller and speaking with more confidence than he had the last time they had been together. Mike was glad that things had worked out well for him. He spoke about Ryan with great affection and it was clear that things were progressing well between them given that they had moved in together. While Mike was happy for Jim, there was a part of him that had to force a smile as well as he was reminded of the life that he was never going to have with Aaron. But there was something else too... something that he knew was dangerous but he could not escape. The old feelings returned, as though they were rising from a tomb in which they had been buried. He dared not give voice to them lest they consume him.

Michelle was delighted as he got ready to go out. She beamed and didn't make any effort to hide her excitement, but she also displayed her mothering side as well, asking him if he was really going to be all right. She fussed over him, but secretly he enjoyed it.

The walk in the park with Jim had done him wonders. To be in such a lush, vibrant world instead of staring out at endless desert reminded him of all that he had missed from home, and even though Aaron couldn't be there to enjoy it as well, Mike was starting to remember the life he had before all of this.

There was a beep from outside and Mike walked out, making his way to Jim's car. Night had fallen in a dramatic sweep of darkness. Two strong headlights cut through the night sky. Even though it was quiet and peaceful there was something that twitched in Mike's mind, something that didn't seem quite right. He had spent so long honing his instincts for danger that he still looked for it, even here.

"Hey, I'm Ryan, it's nice to meet," Ryan said, twisting around in the passenger seat, offering him his hand. It was a strong hand. Mike pushed himself into the back seat, lifting his leg. He could immediately see what had attracted Jim to Ryan. Ryan had exciting eyes and a flair when he spoke. His face was expressive and there was no deception with him at all. Whatever emotions he was feeling were displayed without reservation. There was something both charming and intimidating about this openness.

Mike caught Jim's eyes in the rearview mirror. A jolt of electricity shot through him. The car pulled away as they made their way to the mall. Mike breathed deeply, trying to keep himself calm. He tried to position himself a step or two behind Ryan and Jim, using them as a shield to prevent others from seeing his broken body. The stores were all shut, but the cinema was open and people poured in in waves.

"I'll go and grab the tickets," Ryan said, offering to get them some popcorn and drinks as well.

"Thanks for doing this Jim," Mike said. "If it's all the same to you I won't bother with the popcorn and drinks. I can only really afford the ticket," he said, his voice heavy with shame.

"Mike don't worry about a thing. It's our treat. Just enjoy yourself," Jim said. Mike nodded, although he still felt uncomfortable and strange. He didn't like receiving the charity of others and had to remind himself that it was a friendly gesture rather than anything set out to humiliate him shame him. "I'm glad you came tonight," Jim continued. "I know it's not easy for you to be and out about just yet, but I'm glad we can do something like old times," he said. Mike nodded. The cinema did hold many special memories for him. He and Jim had often come here on the weekends and watched two or three films in a row. Life had been so simple then, with it being easy to while away the hours with nothing else to do and nothing to worry about.

Ryan returned swiftly, brandishing the tickets and two large boxes of popcorn. Jim took the sodas to help and they walked through to the cinema.

"I see they haven't changed the seats," Mike said wryly as he sat down on a hard chair, shaking his head as the fabric seemed to be the same as when he had left.

"I told you that not everything had changed in your absence," Jim grinned. Ryan sat on the far side, with Jim in the middle, and Mike on the left of him, at the aisle so he could spread his leg out. He had to adjust it a few times since people kept threatening to bump into it as they ran up and down the aisles.

"So, Mike, Jim has been telling me that you've had a bit of trouble adjusting being back home. If you ever want to just come round and hang out, get away from your folks a bit, you're welcome around ours. We haven't really had many parties yet, but we want our place to end up being the social hub of the neighborhood where it's always alive with some kind of intrigue and color. I grew up in a quiet home and I never wanted my home to be like that. I want something happening all the time, for there always to be the chance of excitement and adventure."

"Well, maybe not all the time," Jim laughed nervously. Mike noticed the anxious look on Jim's face and wondered how much of this was Jim's idea.

"Yeah, I'm surprised at that. You always hated parties Jim," Mike said.

"Those were high school parties. I'm talking sophisticated affairs where you can have everyone from a king to a pauper in attendance, a special place where there are no rules and everything can be shared in a secret confessional," Ryan lowered his voice and fluttered his long lashes, acting conspiratorial. Jim laughed awkwardly and arched his eyebrows. Mike smiled and nodded, trying to figure out if Ryan was being serious or if everything was a joke to him.

The lights dimmed and the images flickered on screen. Booming sound thundered all around them, and Mike jumped. Tension gripped him in a way that he hadn't expected. The colors were bright, but everything was so enormous and intimidating. Sweat trickled underneath his clothes and his hands were shaking. His throat ran dry and his gaze twisted from right to left. This wasn't how it was supposed to be. This wasn't how he felt in his bedroom, but somehow in the cinema it was different. The film was only ten minutes old, but Mike wondered how he was going to cope with the rest of it. He glanced across. Ryan and Jim were laughing, tossing kernels of popcorn into their mouths, lost in the immersive world. The rest of the crowd joined in. They were of one mind, one body. They laughed together, they gasped together, and none of them seemed to be aware that anything was wrong.

But something was.

Mike could feel it crawling at the base of his skull. It whispered in the back of his mind, but the whisper was drowned out by another deafening sound effect. He had to get out and clear his mind so he could hear himself think. His palms were clammy, and for the sake of Ryan and Jim he tried to hold out for as long as he could, trying to force himself to stay for the rest of the movie, but there came a point where he knew he had to leave. He mumbled an apology and rose, grabbing his cane and walking as quickly as possible toward the rear doors. They seemed so far away. He noticed other people looking at him, mocking him, wondering why he would ever leave now. The world was closing in on him and how were these doors moving away? There was some trick, something was wrong.

Eventually his hand pushed them and they swung open. He breathed, not realizing he had been holding his breath until he left the cinema. The bright lights welcomed him and he pressed himself against the wall, gulping in air. He wiped the sweat from his brow and closed his eyes, wishing that he were better, wishing that he were stronger.

The doors opened again. Ryan and Jim were standing there, looks of concerns on their faces.

"Are you okay?" Jim asked, placing his hand on Mike's shoulder.

"Yeah I... I don't know what happened in there. It was just so loud and I couldn't think straight and it felt like something was wrong. I just had to get out of there. I'm sorry. You two should go back inside and enjoy the rest of the movie. I don't want to spoil the evening for you."

"Hey, this evening was supposed to give me a chance to get to know one of Jim's oldest friends. It's no big deal; the movie wasn't that great anyway. Now come on, there's a place that does great smoothies around here," Ryan said. Mike knew he was lying because he'd seen how much they had been enjoying the movie, but he appreciated it anyway. He flashed Jim an apologetic smile as they moved away from the cinema. Ryan and Jim looped their arms together, while Mike continued to grip his cane.

Ryan ordered them smoothies. While he was at the counter, Mike and Jim had some time alone.

"He's really nice. I can see why you like him," Mike said, "although I don't know if he's really that flamboyant or if he's making a big joke of it all."

"Oh no, that's really him," Jim said with a smile. "He just approaches everything with gusto, or at least that's what he tells me. It's how we met actually. He saw me and came right up to me and told me that I swept him off his feet and that we should go and get a drink. He just says whatever is on his mind, and it's refreshing."

Ryan returned with some colorful smoothies.

"So, come on then Mike, tell me some embarrassing stories about Jim. That's why I'm here after all. I tried asking his parents but they were woefully unprepared to spill the beans. I'm hoping that you have something juicy. I know there are some things he's been hiding from me and I want you to help me get to the truth," Ryan said, smirking. Mike noticed how Jim squirmed, although he didn't know what secrets Jim had.

"I don't know, I mean, there's not much to tell really, although there was that time when we saw like three movies while only paying for one. We had to sneak between the different theatres without them seeing us. By the last one I think they were onto us. The usher followed us into the cinema and we hid down, crouching on the floor," Mike said.

Jim laughed. "Oh God yeah, I still remember that it was sticky," he shook his head and then grimaced, pretending to wipe the ooze off his hands. "And remember that time we actually got told off for laughing so much? I can't even remember the film now," Jim turned to Ryan to explain. "It was such an over-the-top thing that we couldn't help laughing, but apparently the people around us didn't take kindly to this and they started to get annoyed. We didn't realize we were being so loud, and an usher came along to tell us to be quiet."

"Reminds me of that time when we went to that restaurant and I ordered a wedge salad as a starter, do you remember?" Mike said. Jim slapped his hand on the table and wiped a tear of laughter from his eyes.

"I'd forgotten about that!" he exclaimed.

Ryan frowned a little. "What's so funny about a wedge salad?"

Jim and Mike started speaking at the same time, as though they were of one mind. Jim held out his hands and surrendered the story to Mike. "Well, when I saw it on the menu, I assumed it was some kind of salad with potato wedges, and it was supposed to be topped with some mayo and bacon bits. It sounded great, but when they brought it out it was just a quarter of a lettuce with some bacon bits sprinkled on top and a bit of mayo sprayed over it. And it was like five bucks! I wasn't going to pay that for a quarter of a lettuce. Who wants to eat a quarter of a lettuce anyway?"

"So, he ends up calling the waiter over and asking if this is a joke. The waiter stammers and gets flustered and obviously he knew that having lettuce on the menu was stupid, but he couldn't admit it, probably because he'd get fired. So, there he is trying to argue that a quarter of a lettuce is worth five bucks. What made it worse was that the restaurant had a policy of no refunds with this kind of thing, and they just wouldn't budge. The manager had to come over and point to some small print, so we ended up just paying the bill and then leaving to grab a burger elsewhere."

"We never went back to that restaurant again," Mike added, and as he looked at Jim something changed inside him. For a moment he was transported back to a time before all the sorrow had poisoned him, before he could taste nothing but bitterness on his tongue. While before the rest of his life had been achingly distant, it now seemed closer than ever before, as though it was really a part of him and that he was still the person he was before all of this. It was as though Jim was his anchor through the stormy seas of time. Even if Mike were unable to remember what it was like to live in this place, Jim could remember for him. The memories he had were shared ones, and that made them more real.

The night continued in this vein. The smoothies were slurped up, but still they remained at the small table, reminiscing about the past. The stories twisted between them. It was like a relay race; Jim would start something, and then Mike would finish it, and then Jim would add another embellishing detail that Mike had forgotten. It seemed so easy to slip into the past, and it was oh so comforting, as though a blanket had been pulled over him. But at the same time a flame of guilt flickered within, because he knew that while he was having this good time Aaron wasn't having anything. Why should he be able to have all this when Aaron could have nothing? It didn't seem fair, and Mike grew quiet as Jim was telling another story. He offered a weak smile and then suggested that it was time to go home.

They pulled up at Mike's house and Mike thanked them for a good evening. Jim got out of the car as well and walked Mike to his door.

"I'm glad that you came out this evening. It was fun. We should do it again, and like Ryan said, whenever you want to come round and hang out feel free, but there's no pressure. I know that you're still adjusting to being back."

"It was good, thank you," Mike repeated.

"It was fun thinking about the old times," Jim said, his eyes shimmering with something elusive. A lump appeared in Mike's throat.

"It was."

There was a pause between them, a silence that yearned to be filled with something, but neither said what was truly in their hearts.

"I guess I'll see you soon then," Jim said. He motioned to give Mike a hug, but instead settled for a pat on the shoulder. Mike leaned in anyway and rested his head against Jim.

"Thank you," Mike whispered again. He wasn't sure if Jim would ever know how much this meant to him.

***

"How was it?" Michelle asked. Mike looked at the stairs. Usually he would have walked straight up them and hidden himself away in his room, but he could hear the pleading tone in his mother's voice and knew that all she wanted was a chance to connect with her son, to know that he was still a real, living thing and not just a ghost. He nodded and then walked into the kitchen where he leaned against the counter and poured himself a drink. Michelle followed tentatively, as though she was afraid that one wrong move would send him scurrying away like a scared little mouse.

"It was actually really good. I'm glad I went. We spoke a lot about the old days," Mike said.

Michelle's face broke out in a wide smile and her eyes glistened with tears. "I'm so happy to hear that Mike. I had a feeling Jim might have been able to get you out of your room. You and he were always so close."

"Yeah, we were…" Mike said. He swallowed an ache in his throat and licked his lips. It had been a relief to tell Mike what had really happened and why he was so upset, and now he wondered if perhaps it wouldn't be the worst thing in the world to reveal the truth to his mother either. He started to tell his story. His voice was a drawl, heavy with emotion. There were moments when he had to stop and let his emotions settle to stop them from boiling over, but by

77

the end he had told Michelle all about his relationship with Aaron.

Michelle choked on a sob and came to her son, hugging him. Mike braced himself against the emotion. He had kept himself so distant, so isolated since he had been home that he had never allowed himself to surrender to his mother's comfort, but now he dropped his defenses and fell into his mother's arms. Tears flowed between them and the ice in his heart began to melt.

Chapter Eight

Jim's keys made a rattling sound as he threw them in the bowl and made his way to the couch.

"That was a really fun night. Thanks for coming Ryan. I'm sorry that we had to cut the movie short. I didn't realize that he was so sensitive to that kind of thing. I hope you didn't get bored too much when we spoke of old times. I get the feeling that he needed that to try and reconnect to this place and make it feel like home again. Man, there were some of those things that I had completely forgotten about."

"It was nice to have a glimpse into the window of your life before me," Ryan said simply, but there was an edge to his voice that Jim couldn't miss. He slipped to the couch and glanced at the clock, amazed at how late it was. He yawned, but the yawn was cut short as Ryan said something that shocked him.

"When were you going to tell me that you love him?" Ryan asked.

Jim was wide-eyed and his skin crawled as though he was exposed. His throat clenched and his heart skipped a beat.

"What are you talking about?" he tried to keep his voice steady, but he could sense the tremors in it. This was his deepest secret and Ryan had just drawn attention to it as though it was the most obvious thing in the world. Was he truly this transparent or was it just that Ryan was adept at reading him?

"Don't play coy with me," Ryan arched his eyebrows and tried to act playful, although Jim could see the concern in his eyes. "I saw the way you looked at him, and the way you two just fit together like two missing pieces of a jigsaw."

"We're old friends you know. We spent a lot of time together. I guess we just have that kind of rapport."

Ryan studied him. "No, it's more than that. I know these kinds of things when I see them. He meant a lot to you."

"Ryan, that's not-"

Ryan cut him off by raising a hand. "I don't know if you're trying to deny this to yourself or to me, but either way it's not going to work. I know what I saw Jim. I saw two people who have a shared history and genuine affection for each other. The way conversation ebbed and flowed between you... it was as though you shared one mind. You can be honest with me you know. In fact, that's all I ask. I'm hardly some traditional puritan who only believes we can love one person in our lives. It's clear that he means a lot to you and that's wonderful! But I just want to know where I stand. I have some deal breakers in my relationships Jim, and I don't want to live with any doubt that I have to share your heart. So, does he know? Were you two an item before he shipped out?"

Jim felt his world crumbling around him. Ryan had struck at the heart of the matter with a swift stroke, as though he was an expert swordsman displaying his prowess to win the hearts of fair maidens. For a few moments he was agog, scrambling around to find what to say. Instinct told him to deny it all because that had been his habit for so long. For the past, God, decade at least he had buried these feelings within and never allowed himself to embrace them fully. For Ryan to wrench them out like this was torture, and all he wanted was to turn away and put them back where they had been buried.

But he knew Ryan wasn't going to let him. He stood there, tall and lean, wearing an expectant gaze. Ryan was neither cruel or malicious, yet in that moment Jim hated him for this, hated him for forcing him to look at the ugly truth and face something that he had spent so much of his life turning away from.

"I'm with you Ryan," he said weakly.

"I know you are, but that's not what I asked." Ryan sat down beside him and spoke gently. "You need to tell me the truth Jim."

Jim nodded, groaning inside. "Okay, I don't know when it started, but one day I realized that I loved him. It just clicked inside me. We only really had each other at school. Neither one of us took part in any clubs or anything, and the whole thing seemed like a joke to us. So, we hung out whenever we could and I just loved him."

"Did he love you?"

"I don't think so. I don't think the thought ever occurred to him," Jim said, although in truth it hadn't really occurred to him either. Now, especially after hearing about Aaron, Jim did wonder if perhaps he and Mike had had the same feelings and trepidation in sharing them. "I was going to tell him the truth on prom night and lay it all out on the line, but before I could he had something to tell me. That's when he said he was joining the army, and then what I had to say just didn't seem so important anymore."

As Jim spoke, he revisited the pain and the sorrow of that night, slinking home with his heart sunk so deep into his body he wasn't sure it would ever rise again. The world had seemed hollow then, for without Mike what kind of life would he have?

"But that's all in the past Ryan. I promise you. I'm with you now. I haven't seen Mike in years. I have my own life now. We live together."

"But it's not all in the past Jim, because Mike is back."

"Are you going to ask me to not see him again?"

"No, I would never do that, especially because he clearly needs it if he's ever going to adjust to being at home. But I just... I can't be with someone who isn't with me a hundred per cent, okay? I just need to know that this isn't going to end in heartbreak for me, because if it is, I'd rather know sooner than later."

"You don't have to worry about anything Ryan. We're just friends," Jim said, and he hated himself for lying to the man he lived with. Ryan brushed his lips against Jim's mouth, and then Jim rose to get ready for bed. As he did so he tried to push away the stabbing guilt that plagued him. Something had happened during the night. As they had traveled through the past old feelings had returned as well. There were a few moments when he saw the old Mike emerge from the shell of a man he had turned into, and wrapping the old feelings around himself was all too easy for Jim. He hated himself for it because he knew it was complicated and he knew that Ryan didn't deserve this, but he couldn't stop the feelings from flowing. He wasn't even sure if it was still love or if it was just an echo from the past that felt like love. Either way, there was definitely something there, and he was almost afraid to see Mike again lest it return with full force.

***

Michelle had invited Jim around for dinner on Mike's behalf. Jim assumed that Ryan was naturally

82

invited as well, but he decided to go by himself, and even that seemed awkward, but Ryan understood. Things had been a little tense between them since their conversation about Jim's feelings, and Jim was still conflicted. Part of him wondered whether his love for Ryan was as true as he thought, since if it was, then surely he would not still have these feelings for Mike? And as for Mike, well, was it love he felt, or just a longing for days when things were simpler?

Life and emotions were far too complicated and Jim wished there were a simple way out of his anguish.

Michelle had cooked a good spread. There was roasted meat, mashed potato, thick gravy, and crunchy vegetables. Jim had had many meals here, and it was something he always looked forward to as Michelle was always generous with helpings. When Jim remarked on this she blushed and smiled. Hank was sitting at the table as well, and it seemed like a real event. Jim supposed it was. From the hints Michelle had given it didn't seem as though Mike spent much time with his parents despite living under the same roof, but Jim was glad that things were changing, and he was proud to have something of an influence on this.

Hank asked Jim what he had been up to in the intervening years, so Jim told him all about his job. Michelle was fascinated and the conversation seemed to revolve around it. Jim didn't mind. He kept glancing at Mike, who rarely spoke, but he listened, and that was enough. Jim noticed how Michelle and Hank avoided speaking about anything that might have triggered something in Mike. The conversation was always quiet and soft. The topics always safe and light. Jim wondered what it must have been like to always tread so lightly, as though they were surrounded by eggshells.

Dessert was brought out, and after this Jim and Mike went upstairs to be alone. Mike sighed with relief as he sank on his bed. Jim perched on the end, just as they had done in their teenage years.

"Does it ever feel weird, living here again, like you've gone back in time?" Jim asked.

Mike nodded. "It does, and I hate it, but I don't know when I'm going to be ready to leave, or if I ever will. Sometimes I think I'm going to be stuck here for the rest of my life."

"You can't really believe that, can you? There's something out there for you. I'm sure you'll be able to find a job."

"I don't know. The thought of being out there again… it makes me shudder."

Jim's heart went out to him then. There were times when he saw the old Mike, but other times when these new characteristics displayed themselves. The Mike he knew was always courageous and ready to meet adventure, but now he was uncertain and tentative, afraid of all the chaos life could bring.

"It was scary for me too, after college. I was lucky that I fell into a job."

"You weren't lucky Jim, you've worked hard to get where you want to be. You have a good life. Things have worked out well for you and I'm glad. I'm happy for you. Ryan seems like a great guy as well."

"Yeah, he is," Jim said, another pang of guilt flashing inside him. "I enjoyed the other night. It was fun talking about old times."

"I know, it's almost like another life," Mike said, resting his head against the wall. "When I think back to how young we were… man, we did some stupid things didn't we?"

"I guess everyone does. It could have been a lot worse. We could have gotten in a lot more trouble."

"Yeah, Aaron was like that. He told me all these stories of the kinds of things he and his brothers got into and it was wild. Part of the reason why he went into the army was because he wanted some structure and discipline. I think he was afraid that he'd end up doing something that couldn't easily be fixed if he didn't get out of there. I guess in the end it happened anyway…" Mike trailed off and Jim could sense the pain in his words. He wasn't blind to the fact that while his life had progressed and ascended to be this safe, loving thing, Mike's had crashed to the ground like a falling star and now smoldered. Part of him would always be lost to this grief, and it wasn't as though it was even his fault. He hadn't been able to go to the funeral, so he hadn't been able to have any closure.

Suddenly Jim was struck with an idea. He rose from the bed and opened the window.

"What are you doing?" Mike asked.

"I'm sneaking out like old times."

"Where are you going?"

Jim looked back and flashed a smile. "Where are *we* going?" he teased.

"I can't go out there. I can't climb down the tree, not with my leg," Mike said.

"I think you can. Look, it seems to me that a lot of your pain revolves around the fact that you weren't able to say goodbye to Aaron properly, so I think we should go and have a memorial service for him where we can say goodbye. And we should sneak out just for the sake of it, to recapture our teenage spirit."

Mike thought about the matter for a moment and then slowly approached the window. He peered out.

"It never looked this far down before," he said as he gazed at the ground, which lurched before him.

"It's okay, I'm right here with you. I'll help you," Jim said, placing his hand on Mike's shoulder. Their eyes met in the fading twilight and a chord was struck in Jim's heart, as though a mighty bell rang out and its peals trembled through his body and soul.

He took Mike's hand to help him get onto the thick gnarled branch that ran from the bedroom window to the trunk. Mike straddled it and pulled himself closer to the trunk, hugging it closely. Jim grabbed his cane and walked out after him, his footsteps more confident. When their hands met heat flashed through Jim's body, dangerous in all it inspired within him. A fire crackled and embers glowed brightly. A sense of awe filled him that these feelings had persisted through all these years, that they had lain dormant instead of vanishing. Now he knew why none of his relationships had ever worked out, because none of them had been with Mike.

But what did that mean for Ryan?

Jim pushed the thoughts away as he descended the tree, helping Mike down all the way. The fear on Mike's face was apparent. The color drained from his cheeks and he squealed anxiously as he followed Jim to the ground. He leapt the last few feet and Jim caught him. Hands wrapped around Mike's waist and for a brief moment they were intimately close. Jim felt as though life had been torn away from him when Mike stepped away.

***

They went to a forgotten, hidden place of the park that glowed as though it was from a fairytale. The sky was a mix of gold and red, regal in its majesty. They went to a small copse where Jim gathered some brittle wood and dry leaves, making a small pyre. Then, he bent down and quickly made a fire using a trick he had learned as a child. A thin plume of smoke rose, dancing and twisting through the air.

"I'm not really sure how to begin," Mike said.

Jim smiled. "I don't think there are any rules. You don't have to say anything if you don't want to." Jim clasped his hands in front of him and bowed his head respectfully. The small fire crackled gently, the flames offering windows into the past. It seemed to burn through time, and yet some things were more powerful than fire. It couldn't burn away love, after all.

They were silent, and Jim didn't think that Mike was going to say anything, but then he eventually spoke in a voice that was as soft as a whisper and heavy with grief.

"I'm sorry," he began. "I'm sorry that I wasn't able to save you. I'm sorry that it wasn't me instead of you. It should have been me. I'm sorry that we never got to do all the things that we had planned to do. When I joined the army, I was so unsure of my place in the world. I didn't know where I belonged. I'd only ever had one friend and I had left everything behind to try and find myself, and instead I found you.

I knew you were different from the first moment I saw you, and the more time we spent together the more I knew that we shared something special. It would have been so easy for us to not act on our feelings, but I'm glad we took the chance because even though we didn't get as much time as we wanted, we still got some time together. I just wish I got to say goodbye. I'm sorry Aaron, and thank you. Thank you for everything. I'm never going to forget you."

The words disappeared into sobs. Jim walked up to Mike and squeezed his shoulder. At the gesture Mike turned and hugged Jim, burying his head against Jim's collarbone. Jim held the trembling body and thought on the words. It was clear how much Mike and Aaron had meant to each other, but he also knew that love wasn't the kind of thing that was experienced only once during a lifetime. Jim wondered what would have happened if he had taken a chance on his feelings, and this thought was what gripped him as they went back to Mike's house. Mike was solemn after the memorial service, but he thanked Jim for the lovely thought.

"I think it is going to help me move on. You're a good friend Jim. I don't think I realized how much I missed you."

Jim smiled. It was impossible now to stop all of the old feelings from flooding back. Something had begun within him and he was unable to stop it, even if perhaps his better judgment would have told him to shy away. But life was all about chances, all about risk. Four years ago he had kept his lips sealed and his feelings hidden, but it seemed wrong that his mother and Ryan should know the way he felt about Mike without Mike knowing, and he also knew that if he didn't tell Mike now then he never would.

"Mike," he said as Mike was just getting out of the car. Mike turned to face him. Jim continued speaking, knowing if he stopped, he would lose all the drive that commanded him. "I was thinking about what you said earlier, about how we have to be brave and we can't hide our feelings away. There's something I need to tell you, something that I should have told you a long time ago. I... I love you Mike. I loved you back then, and I was going to tell you on prom night, but then you said you were leaving and I thought there was no point in telling you how I feel. And now that you're back, I've realized my feelings haven't really gone away. I tried to convince myself that I don't because it's easier that way, but after tonight I know they're still there and I just... I had to tell you because it's burning up inside me. I don't know what I expect but I just... I needed to tell you."

Jim exhaled deeply after he spoke, feeling better for having shared his feelings. His eyes danced with possibility and abandon filled his heart. He didn't care if he was throwing caution to the wind because it felt exciting. Anything might happen, and the rush of adrenalin thrummed in his ears. Everything was a whirl, and he looked at Mike expectantly, waiting for his reaction, but he was disappointed.

Mike looked stunned. "That's... that's very sweet of you Jim. I just... I'm not sure what I'm supposed to do with that information. I don't even know how I feel about things. I'm still trying to adjust being back here. I love having you as a friend and knowing that I can count on you. You've reminded me that I can still have a life here and what you've done for me tonight is amazing, but anything else I... I just don't know. I'm sorry."

Jim swallowed his heart and rested his hands against the steering wheel. He nodded and looked aghast, feeling foolish for having blurted out his feelings like this. Of course it was the wrong time. "I'm sorry. Yeah. I know. I didn't mean that you had to, you know, say anything. I just wanted to tell you how I feel and felt and... yeah. I'm sorry. I didn't mean to make things awkward it's just been on my mind a lot and Ryan thought that there was something between us the other day and I guess I've just been thinking about it and... yeah... I'm sorry. I guess, well, you should probably call me if you want to hang out again," Jim said.

Mike said nothing as he left the car. Jim gripped the wheel so tightly his knuckles went white, and the engine roared as he sped away, wondering what had possessed him to open up his heart to Mike. And now he was going to have to go home to Ryan, a man who had shown him nothing but affection and devotion, and he was going to have to try and pretend that he could love Ryan wholly and completely.

Chapter Nine

Mike entered the house through the front door, much to the surprise of Michelle.

"I thought you were still in your room. Where did you sneak off to?" she asked, although secretly he thought she was pleased that he had done something like this, something that was more like the old him. Right now though, he was shaken.

"Jim thought it would be a good idea if we had a little memorial service for Aaron."

"Was it?" Michelle asked.

Mike nodded.

"He sounds very special. I'm sorry that I never got a chance to meet him. You know Mike, if there's ever anyone who is special to you like that again you don't have to worry about bringing them around here. I'd be happy to meet them," she said. Mike nodded, but the words that Jim had just spoken haunted him. The confession he had made lingered, and Mike didn't know what to do with it. In this instance it would have been so easy to return to the darkness, to shut himself away in peaceful solitude, but somehow, he knew that wasn't what Aaron would have wanted, and it wasn't something he wanted for himself either. He told Michelle that he wanted to speak to her, and she gladly accepted the offer.

They went into the kitchen. Michelle made some cocoa and they sat close to each other, snacking on some chocolate.

"I know it must have been hard to say goodbye to Aaron today, but I think it's a good step. I don't know if there is an afterlife or not, but I do believe that people can live on as long as we remember them, and I'll be happy to carry the memory of him with you," Michelle said, squeezing his arm. Mike smiled, knowing that she could feel his pain, although she was mistaken in the source of it.

"Actually, I didn't want to talk to you about Aaron. I wanted to talk to you about Jim."

Michelle's face lit up when he mentioned Jim's name. "Ah Jim! It's so good to see him again, and he's done quite all right for himself, hasn't he? It's good to see you two together again. You always were inseparable. You know, after you left he was quite despondent. Sometimes I actually caught him standing out on the other side of the road, looking up at your bedroom window. I always made it clear that he was welcome to come in, but he never took me up on the offer. Eventually he stopped coming around."

"He did?" Mike asked. In all this time he had never truly thought about how difficult it must have been for Jim, especially after what Mike had just learned.

"Oh yes, but I can't blame him really. I feared for both of you when you left. You were together so much. Your friendship got you through those difficult years, but at least you found Aaron so you didn't have to be so alone. And now you have Jim again. I was a little worried that things might be different for you because as life goes on, people tend to change and drift apart, but I'm glad to see that the bond you have hasn't been broken. It's important to have people in life that we can depend on, and Jim is one of those. It warms my heart to know that you're spending time with him because it feels like I'm getting my son back. I know I shouldn't say something like that because you've always been my son and I'll love you no matter what, but when you were shutting yourself away in that room, I was afraid that it would never end. All I've ever wanted is for you to be healthy and happy, and to know that you're going out and spending time with a friend really does warm my heart."

"I don't know how much more time we're going to spend together," Mike said bluntly. Michelle's expression changed and her position shifted, rising up to her full height.

"What happened?" she gasped, afraid for her son once again.

"He told me he loved me," Mike said in a stilted voice. He then went on to explain what Jim had told him. Michelle listened in silence and let out soft sighs.

"He certainly could have chosen a better time to tell you this, but I suppose if it's been on his mind for a while…"

"I don't know what I'm supposed to do Mom. How can I be friends with him now when I know he feels this way? It's going to be so awkward and love has been the farthest thing from my mind. I just wish he hadn't said anything. It would have been so much easier for things to remain as they were, but he had to go and ruin everything."

"Michael, don't you dare say something like that," Michelle only used his full name when she was really disappointed with him, and it made his head snap to attention. "I know it's not what you wanted to hear, but it must have taken a great deal of courage for him to confess his feelings. He's always been a sensitive boy and you shouldn't act like this is something to be ashamed of. You two have been through so much together and, to be honest, there was a part of me that wondered if something like this existed between you two. Is it really beyond the realm of possibility that something could happen?"

"I don't know," Mike twisted his face, "he's with Ryan anyway."

"Mike think about all the time you two spent together. Think about the way you made each other feel. You trusted each other with everything. You spent all your time together. If that's not love then what is? And I don't think it would be the worst thing in the world for you to let your life be touched by love. Now I'm not forcing you to rush into anything or make yourself feel anything you're not sure that you really feel. All I'm trying to say is that you shouldn't close yourself off to the possibility of love. You have been through a lot and you've suffered enough for a lifetime. Isn't it about time that you let something good happen to you? This place doesn't have to be purgatory. You don't have to spin your wheels here and act like life is never going to get any better. There's a man out there who loves you, who has always loved you, and that's not something you should turn away from." She reached out and gripped his hand tightly. "Love is what binds us all together Mike. Please, please don't turn away from this, not right away."

Mike was surprised at the strength of his mother's words and the steel in her eyes. He nodded and promised her that he wouldn't. The words sounded foreign even as they came from his own mouth. He retreated upstairs with much on his mind. There had always been affection between him and Jim, and perhaps if Jim had confessed his feelings things might have been different. But now... here... things were so messy. What was Jim even doing loving him when he had a settled relationship with

Ryan? It didn't make any sense, but Mike didn't want to lose the only friend he had. Despite his initial reluctance he had enjoyed venturing out in the world and feeling connected to other people again. It wasn't a feeling he wanted to lose, but at the same time he just didn't know how to handle something like this. His head thrummed, and to dull the pain he turned on the TV and tried to lose himself in the flashing images, as he had done so many times before. But this time it didn't quite work. This time he couldn't get Jim off his mind.

Chapter Ten

"Do you think I should call him?" Jim asked, gnawing on his knuckles. His leg jiggled with nerves.

"I think you should do whatever you think best dear," Jenny said absently, which wasn't any help to Jim whatsoever.

"I should call him," Jim picked up his cell phone, but then dropped it almost immediately, shaking his head and rubbing his temples. "No, I told him that he should call me if he wanted to hang out. I said what I had to say and I have to leave it. The ball is in his court," he said, although he was trying to convince himself more than anything.

The past week or so had been hectic. After Jim had confessed his feelings to Mike, he hadn't heard anything from the man. He'd returned home to Ryan. As soon as he saw Ryan standing there, he knew he needed to tell him the truth. What followed was a long conversation that ebbed and flowed between an argument and a discussion. Ryan accused Jim of wasting his time and being disingenuous with his feelings. Jim pleaded innocence and said that he was still trying to figure out everything that jumped and danced inside him. It was confusing and all he needed was understanding, but it was in short supply. They had stood in their apartment, which was still in the process of being decorated and fashioned into the perfect home, when they decided that things were coming to an end. Jim had returned to his parent's house and told them all that had happened. It was a messy situation and Jim was afraid that he had lost everything. He had no Ryan, and Mike was being silent. Not that Jim could blame him. There was a time and a place for these things and Jim had just blurted it out after the memorial of someone that Mike cared deeply about. The more Jim thought about it the more he cringed and he wished that he could go back in time and stop himself from making such a fool of himself.

And now he was forced to wait while his heart hung in the balance. Would Mike ever get in touch with him or had Jim pushed him too far? It was for this reason that Jim was hesitant to get in touch with Mike again. Things were awkward already without him running back to Mike, pleading to talk with him, and what was Jim even going to say? Would he just pretend that nothing at all had happened, or did he need to take back what he said? He had made this whole thing about him when Mike was clearly still struggling with settling back into this life. He was selfish and he hated himself for it because he had let down his best friend.

But there was nothing he could do about it now.

"If Mike wants to get in touch with you then he'll get in touch with you, and I'm sure that he will. He probably just needs time. The poor boy has been through a lot and it's not easy to deal with this kind of thing. It's no bad thing for him to want a bit of space. You just have to focus on yourself," his mother said wisely. "And you know, part of taking a risk like this is the knowledge that it might not work out. We hope it will, but it doesn't always work out that way, and you'll have to be prepared for that as well."

"I'm starting to think that it wasn't worth the risk. I messed everything up," his head sank into his hands and he groaned loudly. Jenny chuckled a little and rubbed the back of his head.

"But you should be proud for being honest with yourself. If you hadn't been then you would have gone through life always unsure, and in the end, it would have probably ended with Ryan anyway, or you would have resented yourself for not taking your chance when you could have. It's good character building, and I know that probably doesn't seem like much right now, but it's going to be very valuable in the long run. I remember that you always used to be a shy boy, so afraid of doing anything that might draw attention to yourself. Mike really brought out the best in you and now you're able to follow your heart even when it might be dangerous. I'm proud of you Jim."

She squeezed his hand and he responded with a smile. Well, at least it wasn't all for naught. He had won the pride of his mother and that was something. Perhaps it would turn out for the best in the end, but that didn't much help him in the present moment. And yet as he reflected on his life, he did see how much he had changed, and he liked the man he had grown into.

***

Jim answered the door and saw Mike standing there. He rested his hands on his cane and uncertainty flickered in his eyes.

"Hey," Jim said.

"Hey," Mike replied. "Do you think we could go somewhere to talk?"

A smile played on Jim's lips.

"I think I know the perfect place."

They drove up to lookout point. The sky was a brilliant blue. The road curved away and there were patches of moss nearby that overlooked the city. The place was deserted, as it had been all those nights ago when everyone had been occupied with prom.

"The place seems different," Mike said.

"Yeah, it's kind of lost its luster a little bit over the years. It's sort of a relic of a bygone age now. People go elsewhere for their fun. I guess every tradition has to die. I still like to come here sometimes though. It reminds me of old times," Jim said. They were tentative with each other, dancing around the topic. But at least here they could be alone. They unbuckled their seat belts and gazed out at the twinkling city below, feeling like outsiders again.

"I'm sorry for taking so long to call," Mike said.

"Don't worry about it. I'm just glad you did. And I'm the one who should be apologizing. I didn't mean to dump all of that on you. It was just on my mind and it felt like the right time, but I know I made an error in judgment and it wasn't what you needed to hear. I was selfish and I'm sorry."

"I appreciate that, but you don't have to be sorry. What you said was very kind and it does mean a lot to me. I've been doing a lot of thinking this past week about… well… everything really. I've struggled a lot to adjust to life back here and there was a time when I thought I'd never be able to feel at home again, but you changed that. I need to thank you for that, for being my friend even though all this time has passed and even though I have changed."

"You haven't changed *that* much," Jim said, laughing a little, but Mike wore a solemn expression.

"I have," he said. "And that's what I don't get about all this. You say that you love me, but I just don't see how that's possible. You love the person I was. I'm not that guy anymore. I'm just a mess. I'm scarred, both on the outside and the inside. I can't be around people. I don't know when I'm ever going to be ready to work again. I'm holed up in my parent's house because I can't make it anywhere else. If it weren't for them, I'd be homeless. I'm hopeless Jim. You could do so much better than me. How could you love someone like me?"

Jim was struck by the raw honesty in the question and his heart opened up. At first, he almost laughed because it seemed so ridiculous that Mike didn't understand, but as Jim searched Mike's eyes it was clear that he actually wanted an answer to the question.

"Mike, I don't just love the memory of you. All these feelings came flooding back as we started spending time together again. I realized how much I missed you and how much you meant to me. You always made me a better person, and you still do. You understand me like nobody else and when I'm with you I know that I don't have to pretend to be anyone else. You know it destroyed me when you left. I could tell you had your heart set on leaving so I didn't think it was my place to beg you to stay, but I wish I had. It took me a long time to get used to life without you, but I never really let myself move on. When I heard that you were home something awakened inside me and I had to see you again. And the way you spoke about Aaron... it made me realize that it's the way I feel about you. I don't expect you to feel the same way, but I love you because you're everything to me. You always have been and I'm pretty sure that you always will be too. You're not a mess Mike. You've just been through hell. This doesn't define you. This pain isn't who you are."

"But it is a part of me."

"Yes, it is," Jim agreed. Mike wore a thoughtful look.

"And what about Ryan?"

Jim arched his eyebrows and leaned against his door, sighing heavily. "Well, that's in the past. I told him what I said. I thought it best to be honest with him and, well, it took all night but eventually we decided to break up. So, I'm back living with my parents now. To be honest I'm not as upset about it as I thought I would be. There's a part of me that always knew we weren't suited to each other. I mean, he liked the idea of having parties all the time and being this outgoing couple that were always involved in other people's lives, and that's just not me. I prefer the quiet life." He smirked as he looked at Mike.

"So, we're now 24 and we're both still living with our parents, we don't really have any friends apart from each other, and we're out here at Lookout Point. Have we actually grown up or are we stuck in some kind of time loop?" he joked.

"It's good to hear you joking again," Jim said. The tension had cleared a little. The air was quiet. There was still much left unspoken. Jim glanced at Mike. They held their gazes. Jim felt a simmering heat rising within him.

"What happens next?" he asked, his voice catching in his throat. The emotions inside him were deadly and he worried that his fragile world was going to shatter. Mike had his future hanging in the balance.

"I don't know Jim. That's what I've been trying to tell you. I just don't know anything. The world is scary for me right now. Every time I think of the future, I feel scared and uncertain. The only time I feel able to cope with anything is when I'm with you."

Jim's heart pitched. "Then doesn't that tell you something?" he asked. When Mike didn't answer he continued. "Mike, when we were younger, I was afraid of everything but you were the one who pushed me. You were the one who made me feel confident. And when you were gone, I thought about what you'd tell me or how you'd act to combat the fear, and it worked. You say that you've changed, but I'm not the same as I was and a lot of who I am today, is because of your influence. And now I feel as though I can return the favor. I can help you rediscover who you are because I've kept pieces of you in my heart all this time."

Mike looked as though he was going to say something else, and Jim was afraid that he was always going to have to fight for his feelings. Mike licked his lips and they parted. He caught Jim's gaze, but then seemed to throw caution to the wind. Jim felt the sweetness of love bursting against his lips, as though he had just bitten into a succulent fruit. His eyes closed and a hazy feeling settled upon his mind as he drowned in the kiss. Mike's lips were firm yet tender, everything he had always dreamed them to be. Faraway music rang out in his mind and his body tingled all over, his toes curling in sweet anticipation of what was to follow.

Chapter Eleven

Mike had thrown caution to the wind. Over the past week he had been thinking long and hard about his place in the world and his feelings for Jim, coming to the conclusion that he only truly felt alive when he was around Jim. And when Jim had opened his heart, Mike knew that his love was born from something deep and genuine, and that it reflected something within his own spirit. There was one thing that Mike hadn't confessed to Jim; that when he was in the army, he and Aaron had been speaking about the people they had left behind. Mike had spoken about Jim and Aaron had instantly though that they were lovers. Mike had reacted with surprise, but in that moment, he realized how strongly he had felt for Jim.

And now he could ignore it no longer.

They had moved from the car to a mossy, secluded spot that was hidden from any prying eyes. They sank into each other, nervous hands peeling away restrictive clothes. It felt strange and natural all at the same time. Their kisses were fervent, each one of them a burst of fire that radiated heat all over their bodies. Their tongues danced. Low, guttural growls rippled out from them in quaking waves, carrying their emotions. When flesh met flesh there was an outcry of wonder and awe. Their teenage bodies had matured into masculine, muscled temples. Eager fingers slid over hard angels, feeling the tight sinews and the taut outlines of bodies primed for love. Jim lay back and pulled Mike down with him. Their arms wrapped around each other and their legs were entwined. It was impossible to tell where one of them ended and the other began. Their kisses were endless and deep. Mike felt Jim running hands through his hair and then down his back. Mike trailed kisses down Jim's neck and across his chest, feeling the beating heart trembling underneath the supple skin.

They enjoyed the taste of each other and they breathed deeply, growing intoxicated in each other's musky scent. Nature around them was soft and lush, while their bodies were steaming with desire, hard and hot, as though they would scorch the world around them. Tight knots twisted in Mike's stomach as emotions warred within. It was oh so difficult to allow himself pleasure and happiness, but it was a fight he did not have to fight alone. Jim was a steadfast ally, trailing slithering fingers down his back, exploring his body to find the sweet spots that were hard to find.

Their love had flourished many moons ago, before either of them knew what it was. Their love was soulful and deep, as pure as the moon that hung in the sky like a silver lantern, or the crystal rivers that surged across the land. It was eternal and ethereal, blossoming from the mind and heart first before touching their bodies, and now this final act took place that sealed their love. Mike was in awe of Jim's body and was almost surprised at how natural it was to fall into him. Their hands roamed eagerly and easily across the expanse of flesh, as though there was nothing more natural in the world than being with each other. Their lips crashed against each other and great waves of pleasure came through them in torrents. Their hearts soared as they stripped themselves of their last clothes, tossing them away into the small mound of modesty that sat beside them.

Their gazes drifted down at the same time, both of them coated in lust as they looked at the arousal on display. Their hands moved on instinct, mirrors of each other. Fingers curled around taut skin and started to stroke smooth tips. Veins popped and sweat prickled on their skin. Fervent breaths passed through lips and the world seemed to tremble underneath their aching, yearning bodies.

Breath swirled into one as they pressed their foreheads together and shared sweet kisses, interrupted by anguished moans. Mike could feel his blood stirring as they fell into an easy and natural rhythm. It was as though they had been made for each other, perfectly fitting, perfectly responding, perfect in every way. Mike closed his eyes as his mind cracked. It had been so long since he had been touched like this, so long since he had even attempted to pull himself out of his mire of despair with an intimate caress, but with Jim anything seemed possible. He was the man who could rescue him, who could save him from the tragedy of his own soul and pull him back from the brink of the abyss.

He was the one who could make everything better.

And he wanted to show him how much he appreciated it. Mike kissed Jim hard before he slid over his body and descended down the long torso, the air getting thicker and hotter until his tongue wrapped around the warm, tight flesh of Jim's manhood. Mike opened his mouth to welcome Jim in, while also making sure to wet his fingers. The moss was cool and soft underneath, but everything about Jim was hard. Saliva flowed down, drenching him, inch after inch disappearing into Mike's mouth. Jim's head arched back, and the rest of his body followed. As Mike clamped his lips tightly around the shaft, he delved into Jim with deft fingers.

The touch came as a surprise for Jim who gasped and groaned and writhed as Mike slid his slender finger inside Jim, all wet inside the tightness, rubbing and caressing Jim's most intimate area, all while Mike continued to make love to him with his mouth. He glanced up and saw how groggy Jim looked, and Mike let out a satisfied moan as he knew he was making Jim feel good. Every twitch of his finger was met with a burst of pleasure from Jim, until he felt the tension rippling and building. Mike sucked greedily, wanting it all for himself, the need to feel close to someone, needing to feel complete. In one glorious moment heat filled his mouth and settled on his tongue. Jim cried out, his frantic shriek rising through the air, drifting over the city below. The ecstasy made him tremble, and he was covered in prickling sweat.

Mike rose, extricating himself, licking his lips of the last remnants of Jim's lust. He groaned as Jim pulled him down in another deep kiss and rolled him on his back. Jim's eyes were cloudy and his mouth hung open as he returned the favor. Mike watched and every muscle in his body tensed as he felt the joy that came with a sweet mouth making sweet love to him. He tore up grass as pleasure flashed within, and all he could think about was all the time they had wasted in their teenage years.

Why had they done anything else when they could have been doing *this*?

But everything was burned away by the intense sensations that careened through his body. Jim pulled his mouth away, a line of saliva extending and dragging back as he did so. Mike groaned as he looked at his erection, coated in saliva, before Jim straddled him. Mike's hands wrapped around Jim's waist as he felt the comfortable weight of the man settle on him. His erection disappeared into tight, welcoming darkness, and suddenly all the distance between them had disappeared.

They were one.

They were complete.

They were everything.

Mike gazed up in awe at Jim's beautiful body, long and lean and slender. Groping hands ran over Jim's body, feeling the warm sheen of sweat and the powerful beating heart. With every thrust he reclaimed his honor, his strength, his confidence. The very ground rumbled beneath him. The sensations ran rampant in his body, an unstoppable stampede of delight and desire that had been threatening to burst free for so long. Jim draped himself over Mike, burying his head against Mike's neck. Hot breaths crashed against him, their bodies writhed together, and it was as though they moved as one. Mike clung to him as though Jim was the only hope he had left.

Perhaps he was.

Anguished moans were music to Mike's ears. The pliable flesh under his hands felt like a part of himself. Their lovemaking was electric and it was made even more sensual by all the layers of history they had shared with each other. Kisses scorched Mike, and through his blurred vision he saw paradise. Terse moans escaped Jim's lips, and with this anguished torment on his face he had never looked more beautiful to Mike's eyes. They were breaking through the last layer of intimacy, reaching a new stage of their relationship that promised so much joy and wonder.

Tremors rippled through Mike's body, each one growing in intensity until it felt as though lightning bolts were lancing through him. He gasped and groaned as pleasure sang through his body, until it all came flowing out in one burst of orgasmic delight.

Time seemed to stand still as they held each other, shaking and shuddering as they braced themselves against the sensations that enthralled them. Mike looked up to the sky, bright and blue, and for the first time in a long time it seemed as though everything was clear. There were no clouds in the sky, and he was with a man he loved. He glanced around him and the comforting trees and the vivid colors of nature. It was a far cry from the dusty, monochrome desert that had cursed his mind for so long.

He was home. He was finally home.

He kissed Jim and then he ended up breaking into tears as the final walls of his grief came tumbling down. Jim didn't say anything to him, not yet, he seemed to understand that Mike just needed to get this out of his system. They held each other as the breeze drifted over their bodies.

Theirs had been a love years in the making, but now that they had found each other again they were never going to let each other go. When Mike opened his heart to the thought of loving Jim, it was one of the few things that didn't fill him with fear. He kissed Jim's palm as Jim sought to wipe away Mike's tears. Then there was a smile, and a laugh.

Yes, Mike was home after all this time, and he could finally put this all behind him.